FROM DAREDEVIL
TO DEVOTED DADDY

BY
BARBARA McMAHON

MILLS
BOON

First published in Great Britain 2011
by Mills & Boon, an imprint of Harlequin (UK) Limited,
Eton House, 18-24 Paradise Road, Richmond, Surrey TW9 1SR

© Barbara McMahon 2011

ISBN: 978 0 263 22083 4

Harlequin (UK) policy is to use papers that are natural, renewable and recyclable products and made from wood grown in sustainable forests. The logging and manufacturing process conform to the legal environmental regulations of the country of origin.

Printed and bound in Great Britain
by CPI Antony Rowe, Chippenham, Wiltshire

"Would you read me a story tonight?" little Alexandre asked Matt, slipping his hand into the man's larger one.

It was startling. The child was without pretension. He said whatever came into his mind. Holding his hand, Matt was swept away with a feeling of protectiveness toward the boy.

How unfair life had been, losing his father when so young. Who would teach him how to be a man?

The sun had set only moments before. Twilight afforded plenty of light to see. The soft murmur of wavelets against the sand was soothing. Stars had not yet appeared but undoubtedly would before they reached the inn. With Alexandre between them, each holding one of his hands, Matt thought how like a family they must appear.

The thought came more and more frequently. He railed against it. He was on holiday. That was all. Looking over at Jeanne-Marie, he was struck by her air of serenity. Content with her life, happy with her child, she cast a spell over him. He wanted that serenity, that contentment.

Barbara McMahon was born and raised in the south USA, but settled in California after spending a year flying around the world for an international airline. After settling down to raise a family and work for a computer firm, she began writing when her children started school. Now, feeling fortunate in being able to realise a long-held dream of quitting her 'day job' and writing full time, she and her husband have moved to the Sierra Nevada mountains of California, where she finds her desire to write is stronger than ever. With the beauty of the mountains visible from her windows, and the pace of life slower than the hectic San Francisco Bay Area where they previously resided, she finds more time than ever to think up stories and characters and share them with others through writing.

Barbara loves to hear from readers. You can reach her at PO Box 977, Pioneer, CA 95666-0977, USA. Readers can also contact Barbara at her website: www.barbaramcmahon.com

CHAPTER ONE

THE SOFT SIGHING of the sea as it kissed the shore should have soothed Jeanne-Marie Rousseau, but it did not. She stared at the expanse of the Mediterranean sparkling in front of her. The sun was high overhead in a cloudless sky. The sweep of beach at her doorstep was pristine white, dotted here and there with sun worshippers on colorful towels. To a stranger, it appeared a perfect relaxing retreat. Off the beaten track, St. Bartholomeus was an ideal spot for those seeking respite from the hectic frenetic pace of modern life. To live here year-round would be the dream of many.

To Jeanne-Marie, it was home. Sometimes joyful, but today it held a lingering hint of sadness.

Today was the third anniversary of her husband's death. She still missed him with an ache that never seemed to ease. Intermingled with that was anger, however, at the careless way he'd treated life—risking his safety every time he went climbing. Now, not even thirty, she was a widow, a single mother and the owner of an inn in a locale that was thousands of miles from her family. She shook her head, trying to dispel her melancholy thoughts. She had much to be grateful for and her choice of residence was hers to make. She shouldn't second-guess her decision over and over. But sometimes she just plain missed American food, family discussions and longtime friends she saw too infrequently.

Yet this small strip of land reminded her so much of Phillipe, she couldn't bear to leave it. They'd spent several holidays together, enjoying the sea and exploring the small village. Or just sitting together on the wide veranda and watching the sunset, content to be together, never suspecting it wouldn't last forever.

And for him there had been the added attraction of Les Calanques, the cliffs that offered daily climbing challenges to men and women from all over Europe.

Her son, Alexandre, was napping. She was alone with her memories and homesickness. She took a moment to sit on the veranda, remembering happier days. The worst of her grief had long passed. Now she could think about their life together, mourn his death and get on with the practicalities of living.

She would have returned to America after Phillipe's death, but she wanted her son to know his grandparents. Alexandre was all Phillipe's parents had of their only child, except for the photographs taken through the years. Her own parents came to visit annually. They spent lots of time via computers between their trips. And they had six other grandchildren. The Rousseaus only had Alexandre.

And it wasn't as if she didn't love France. It had been her lifelong desire when younger to attend school here and maybe even work for a while. She'd not planned on falling in love with a dashing Frenchman. But love had won out and she'd been living in France for more than a decade now. Those first years of marriage had been so marvelous.

What prompted a man to risk limb and life time and again just for thrills? she asked herself for the millionth time. Challenging himself, he'd so often called it. Scaling mountains with flimsy ropes and gadgets to minimize damage to the rock. As if a mountain would care.

Living with a loving family was enough for her. She'd never understood Phillipe's passion, though he'd tried often enough to enlist her in it. Idly she remembered the trips around Europe, always with a mountain to climb as the destination. The few times she'd tried it, scared and inept, but wanting so much to be with him, she'd only caused him to become impatient and demanding. It had ended up being better for him to go on his own and leave her to her own devices.

She swung her gaze to the right—Les Calanques, the limestone cliffs that afforded daily *challenges* to those who liked free climbing. The spectacular scenery of the sea and coast viewed from the cliffs added to their attraction. Of all the places for her to end up—where rock climbers from around the world came. Or at least those who didn't want to stay in Marseilles for the nightlife. It was quiet as a tomb in St. Bart most nights.

Phillipe had been a dedicated climber, not for him the wild parties that could impair performance the next day. Many shared his philosophy.

She was grateful for that, she thought, idly studying the play of light and shadows on the nearby cliff. Not every single mother had the means to earn a living and remain with her son full-time. And realistically she knew not everyone who went climbing fell to his death. It still remained a mystery to her why people dared life and limb to scale a cliff.

Well, there were other things in life she didn't understand. Her moment of introspection was over. Now it was time to get ready for the influx of guests arriving in the next few hours. Seven new reservations would fill her small inn. Business boomed in the summer months, with rarely a single room vacant more than one night. She was frugal and thrifty and managed her money well. While not wealthy by any means, she and her son were definitely comfortable.

She wanted fresh flowers in each of the rooms when her guests arrived. And she'd replenish the flowers in the rooms of those who had already checked in a couple of days ago. All the rooms had already been cleaned and made up with fresh linens. Last-minute touches remained. She'd deal with bittersweet memories another time. She had guests to prepare for.

Two hours later Jeanne-Marie perched on the high stool behind the mahogany counter at the side of the lounge and looked across the open room. Comfortable sofas and chairs were grouped for conversations. Her son played happily in the sunny spot near one of the open French doors. His two small cars and toy truck gave him endless hours of entertainment. Later, after the last guest had checked in, she'd take him for a swim. The sun was lower in the sky now, flooding the front of the inn, making it just a bit too warm, but she had not yet lowered the outdoor curtains that shaded the wide veranda. She wanted the guests' first impression of the inn to be the best and it looked beautiful when lit by the sun. Every speck of wood glowed with polish. The marble floor gleamed without a trace of the sand that was the bane of her existence. The comfy furnishings begged for travelers to sit and rest. The lounge chairs on the wide veranda in front beckoned with the view of the sea.

She heard a car and looked expectantly to the front. Only her solo male guest remained to check in. Once that was taken care of, she'd be fairly free for the rest of the day.

Glancing out of one of the floor-to-ceiling French doors that lined the front of the inn, she waited. Several were open for the afternoon breeze. She could hear the car door shut, the crush of footsteps on the gravel.

He stepped into view, but instead of coming directly into the inn, he turned on the veranda to survey the sea, then the cliffs that rose to the right.

The counter was set to one side, unobtrusive, not easily seen from the veranda—but offering her a perfect view of the man. He carried himself with an arrogant assurance that usually rubbed her the wrong way. Frenchmen thought highly of themselves. Though this man had reason to. He was a bit over six feet, with broad shoulders, long legs. His dark hair shone in the afternoon sunshine; cut short, it still couldn't disguise the hint of curl. She'd bet he'd been adorable as a child—and all the fawning over him had probably gone straight to his head.

She checked her reservation information. No wife or child with him. Was he married? Or too busy being the superlative male to settle for any one woman? From her vantage point, she could admire as long as she wished. He wouldn't see her.

The soft-sided suitcase he carried wasn't large. He had booked the room for a week. As she watched him turn to study the cliffs along the sea's edge, she knew with certainty he'd come to scale them. She could picture him on the cliffs—his fit and trim body easily meeting the demands of muscles and sinews as fingers lifted his body, toes found infinitesimal crevices to wedge in until he stretched out for another handhold.

She straightened the sign-in card, placing the pen

across it, and waited. Despite her best intentions, she couldn't look away. His shoulders were wide, his arms looked well defined. Upper body strength was a must for those who challenged the face of unforgiving stone. When he turned to step into the inn, she caught a glimpse of his firm lips and strong jaw. His dark eyes scanned the area and rested for a split second on her son. With a hint of a frown, he looked around and found her.

The assertive way he strode across the lounge held her attention. Confident, assured, here was a man used to dealing with life and coming out on top. His clean-shaven jaw was firm, hinting at stubborn determination. His dark eyes flashed appreciation when he saw her and she felt more conscious of being a woman than at any time in the past several years. She wished she had taken time to brush her hair and freshen her lipstick.

Foolishness, she chided herself as she watched him approach. A small skip of her heart surprised her. He was just a guest. No one special. Just amazingly handsome. Curiosity rose. She wondered what he did for a living—he could have been a film actor or male model—except he looked too unaware of his looks to trade on them.

"Bonjour," he said.

"Monsieur Sommer?" she asked, refusing to let herself be captivated by the rugged masculinity, the deep voice or the slight air of distance that enveloped him. When he met her gaze, his dark eyes hid secrets, hinted at pain. That surprised her. Who was he? She wanted to know more.

"You have my reservation," he said. His voice was melodious, deep and rich.

Looking down she couldn't help imagining that voice in her ear at night, telling secrets or talking of love.

"Of course." She slid the card forward for him to sign as every sense went on alert. She was not a woman to have fantasies. Where were those images coming from? She caught a whiff of his aftershave and it caused an involuntary reaction of longing. Too long alone, that's all. Squelching her reactions, she kept her gaze on his hands as he boldly scrawled his name. They were strong, scarred here and there, which only made him more interesting. His attire suggested a businessman, his manner a wild and freely roaming adventurer. Curiosity rose another notch despite her best intention. She usually had little curiosity about her guests. But this man had her intrigued in spite of herself.

"Can you recommend a good place for dinner?" he asked, laying down the pen.

"Le Chat Noir," Alexandre said, coming to stand near the man. "Hi, I'm Alexandre. I live here."

Next to him, her son looked so small. He was already five and growing like crazy, but had a long way to go if he would ever be as tall as Matthieu Sommer.

He looked down at Alexandre, staring for a long moment before saying, "And is that a very good place?"

Her son smiled and nodded emphatically. "Whenever we go out for a treat we eat at Le Chat Noir. It's Mama's favorite."

"Then it must be good. The women, they always know the best places," Monsieur Sommer said gravely.

Alexandre beamed at his response.

Jeanne-Marie was pleased that the man had made the effort to take her son seriously. Alexandre was definitely in need of a male role model. She wished her brother Tom lived nearby. Or her father. Or her cousins. He had his grandfather, of course, but he was so much older and beginning to find a small boy taxing to be around for long.

Matthieu looked back at her. "So, your favorite?" he asked.

"*Oui*. It is excellent and affordable. You might wish to try Les Trois Filles en Pierre. It has a magnificent view of the three stone formations they call the maidens. I assume you're here to climb." She tried to keep her tone neutral, but knew a hint of curiosity crept in.

"I am. I hear the cliffs are challenging and the views incomparable." He studied her for a moment, his head tilted slightly. "Any recommendations?"

She shrugged. "Don't kill yourself."

"My dad fell off a mountain." Alexandre obviously wanted to chime in. Jeanne-Marie wished she hadn't spoken. "He would have taught me to climb mountains. Do you know how?"

"It was a long time ago, Alexandre. I'm sure Monsieur Sommer will be extra careful. We don't tell our guests our family situation," she said gently.

Matthieu Sommer inclined his head once, his gaze moving from her to her son and back again. She wondered what was going through his mind.

"I've given you room six. It's a corner room with a view of Les Calanques." She handed him a key and gestured to the wide stairs along the wall. "To the top and left," she said.

"*Merci.*" He lifted his bag with no effort and soon was lost from sight.

Jeanne-Marie sighed a breath of relief. Meeting her disturbing new guest had caused dozens of emotions to clamor forth. She preferred families with small children to sexy single men who believed they could conquer the world. Especially when just looking at them affected her equilibrium. Too long alone, that's all.

What caused the pain that lurked in his eyes? Why had he come to quiet St. Bart when she'd expect a man like him to choose a luxury place in Marseilles?

She studied the registration card for a long moment, as if his name and address could give her any insights. Sighing in defeat, she filed the card and tried to put her latest guest out of her mind.

Rene, the student who worked evenings, would arrive soon. She'd give him an update on their guests and then be free to take Alexandre for that swim. As she waited for Rene to arrive, her thoughts returned to Matthieu Sommer. He looked to be about thirty-five. Too old not to be married. Maybe his wife didn't share his climbing enthusiasm. That Jeanne-Marie could understand. But when Phillipe had gone climbing, she usually went along and stayed in the village or town nearest the mountain to enjoy the local amenities and be near him when he wasn't climbing. So, was the delectable Frenchman single or just vacationing solo?

Matt Sommer entered room six and glanced around as he tossed his bag on the bed. It was spacious, with high ceilings, windows that went to the floor and a view that didn't quit. Fresh flowers brightened the dresser. He took note of the efforts the innkeeper had gone to, but she could have saved her time. A room was merely a place to sleep for him. When he could sleep, that was.

He crossed to the window and gazed at the cliffs he'd come to climb. A friend had recommended they challenge themselves with Les Calanques, but Paul had wanted to stay in Marseilles, and Matt knew that meant constant party time at night, not at all conducive to serious climbing in the morning. Man against nature, with unforgiving demands that allowed no room for error. He did it to escape. For a short while, his mind freed from the past, he'd pit his skill against the rocks. Brief respites from the unrelenting memories. He was prudent enough when climbing to know he wasn't trying to get killed. But if something happened, so be it. It would be no more than he deserved.

He'd booked the room in this quiet village for a week and planned to do some free climbing with or without Paul. His friend was welcome to the nightlife in Marseilles. Spring was a quiet time at the vineyard. For the next week he was on his own. No one from his family knew where to find him. He'd instructed his PA to contact him only in the case of an emergency—a real emergency.

He studied the rocky crags for a long moment, then turned to survey the space he would inhabit for the next few days. Clean and fresh were the adjectives that sprang to mind. The bed was piled with pillows and a duvet with a pristine white cover. The sheers at the windows billowed slightly in the sea breeze. He could leave the windows open at night and hear the soft lapping of waves. The sun shone in, below the angle of the roof. It could get warm if closed up, but the proprietress obviously knew how to cater to her clientele. The room was charming with local artwork on the walls and two comfortable chairs near the side windows. He sank into one chair and regarded the bed for a moment. If he let himself, he could imagine what Marabelle would have thought of the room. But he wouldn't give in. She was gone. Yet he knew she'd have found the place charming and been delighted to be staying by the sea.

Pushing himself up, he made quick work of putting

his clothes away in the armoire against one wall. Time to explore the small town and maybe pick up some information on the best climbs. The small village nestled in one of the inlets of Les Calanques had appeared quaint enough as he'd driven through. Originally a fishing village, it had opened up to tourists some decades ago, yet still retained its roots. The main part of town flanked the marina and hugged the curving inlet.

The inn was older than he'd expected. How had the young widow become its owner, he wondered. She was pretty and friendly enough. A necessary attribute of an innkeeper, he was sure.

Madame Rousseau seemed far too young to be widowed. Not that there was a certain age that made it suitable. Her son was cute. Did she realize how lucky she was? He'd give anything if his son were still alive.

Matt's own son had burned in the car crash that had killed both him and his mother. A car Marabelle had been driving when Matt should have been at the wheel. He fought the anguish. Nothing would ever ease the pain. The rest of his family had rallied around, but couldn't get through to him much as they tried. No one understood. They offered platitudes, but no one had experienced the same kind of loss. The kind that ripped a heart into shreds and never relented.

The woman downstairs might understand. To a degree. How did she cope?

He wondered if the innkeeper's family had offered the same platitudes when her husband had died. Had it helped? Or had she just wanted everyone to go away and leave her alone with her grief?

Not that he cared. So she was pretty. Marabelle had been beautiful. Love had come swiftly and ended in an instant.

He was here to try the kind of activities he'd once loved—and to forget, if only for a few hours at a time.

"Time to get ready for dinner," Jeanne-Marie called to Alexandre later in the afternoon.

"I don't want to," he said, scuffing along at the water's edge. His small footprints on the wet sand made her smile. One day he'd be taller than her and his footprint would be larger, too.

She joined him and ruffled his hair. "Too bad. We need to eat soon or you'll be finishing dessert in your jammies."

He laughed, clutching his cars close. "We can't eat in our jammies. Can we eat at Le Chat Noir? I'm hungry for some of their food."

"I had planned salad and soup for dinner." Jeanne-Marie gathered their towels, slipping on the cover-up over her bathing suit for modesty's sake. She didn't bother with her shoes; they'd brush their feet off on the veranda and scoot to their quarters.

"Please, Mama. It's a special day. The inn is full, I heard you say. And that's always a good thing."

It was her turn to laugh at his mimicking what she'd said to her friend Madeline. "Yes, it is a good thing. So perhaps we could celebrate with dinner out. But not until you wash that sand off your feet and change into dry clothes!" He didn't even know it was the anniversary of his father's death. She was glad in one way, but mourned how little Alexandre would ever remember about his father. Phillipe had loved him so.

With a yell of glee, he took off running toward the inn. Jeanne-Marie followed, keeping enough behind to let him win. They stomped on the veranda and brushed the worst of the sand from their feet. Alexandre scampered into the lounge and through to the back where their quarters were. She wished she could motivate him this way all the time. She nodded to the student staffing the front desk. Jeanne-Marie relished the few free hours each day Rene's being here gave her.

"Everything okay?" she asked.

"Quiet as ever," Rene responded. He was a bit of a bookworm and always had some book in his hand. Yet he could handle requests with efficiency and expediency. Probably to keep time away from reading to a minimum.

"We're going out for an early dinner," she said.

He nodded, returning to his book.

By the time Alexandre had had a quick rinse and was into fresh clothes and she'd showered, it was after six. Most people in town didn't eat this early, but she liked him in bed by eight, so an early dinner was their norm. Walking down the sidewalk to the heart of the village, the sea to their right, she relished the lingering warmth of the afternoon. It was only early May, but warm enough to swim or lie in the sun as the tourists did. Their little town would fill up before the end of the month. Then for the rest of the summer the town would be transformed from the sleepy fishing village to a fast and furious tourist spot as it expanded to its limit with visitors from all over.

When they reached Le Chat Noir, Jeanne-Marie reached for the door handle just as Alex yelled, "There's one of our guests!"

Glancing up, she saw Matthieu Sommer almost upon them. She caught her breath again at the sight of him. He was definitely walking their way. Tentatively she smiled as she pulled on the door. He'd obviously taken Alexandre's recommendation.

He reached around her, put out his hand to catch the door and gestured for them to enter ahead of him.

"I'm taking your advice and trying this place for dinner," he said as they stepped into the restaurant.

After the sunshine, it took a minute for her eyes to become used to the dimmer illumination. She nodded while holding on to Alexandre's hand. "I think you'll enjoy it."

"Are you going to eat with us?" her son piped up.

"No," she said quickly. Then realizing how rude it sounded, she gave Monsieur Sommer a shaky smile. "I'm sure Monsieur Sommer would not be interested in sharing a table with a five-year-old."

He inclined his head slightly. "I'm not the best company," he said.

Jeanne-Marie nodded and turned to the maître d' as he greeted her.

"Just you and Alexandre?" he asked.

"Oui." She glanced at her guest. "Enjoy your dinner." She was not disappointed he chose not to eat with her. She and her guests rarely mixed. And a businessman here to climb would not be interested in the chatter of a little boy. Still, she wished he'd overridden her comment and said he'd like to eat with her, with them. Though, she'd have been a nervous wreck before the first course.

She and Alexandre were seated at one of the best tables on the patio, the place almost empty. Only two other tables were occupied and far enough away that Jeanne-Marie couldn't hear the occupants, who were talking quietly.

Opening the menu, she took a moment to study the items, already knowing what she and Alexandre always ordered, but looking anyway.

A moment later Matthieu Sommer was seated at a table nearby. Suddenly aware of his presence she tried to keep her eyes on the menu. Fortunately he'd been seated with his back toward her, so she wouldn't have to look up and find him watching her. But she couldn't help taking a glance his way now and then. What was it about him that intrigued her so much? He wasn't particularly friendly. *Keep your distance* was more like the vibe he sent out. Granted, he was a handsome man, but arrogant. She didn't know if she liked him or not, but he certainly had captured her interest.

"I want the chicken," Alex said, kicking his feet against his chair.

"As always. And I'll have the quiche."

"As always," he mimicked, grinning up at his mother.

Jeanne-Marie closed the menu and put it on the table. She glanced at Matthieu Sommer studying his menu. Wistfully she wished she'd asked him to join them. Not that he'd want to spend his meal with strangers. But during the meal she might have discovered more about him. And even realized they had nothing in common so this aberration of interest would fade.

Had he joined them she would probably have ended up as tongue-tied as a teenager facing a major crush. Yet, it must be lonely to eat alone. She debated asking him to join them now, but in the end decided to leave things as they were.

When their order had been taken, Alexandre brought out his small cars and began playing with them on the table. Jeanne-Marie was glad of the distraction. She had to stop staring at her newest guest. Once his order had been taken, he began to look at brochures he'd brought with him. She suspected they were the ones offered at the inn. One touted the shopping in the little fishing village, tourist places all. Another gave an overview of Les Calanques. And a third was one from a local sport shop that catered to climbers.

Alexandre looked up. "Will I be able to take my cars when I go to school in September?" he asked.

"Probably not. You'll need to pay attention in class so you learn all you can."

And she needed to pay attention to her son, and ignore the man sitting so enticingly close.

When their meal arrived, Jeanne-Marie devoted her attention to helping Alexandre with his food and eating her own. She couldn't help notice when Matt's dinner was served. And that he finished at the same time they did. The place was still scarcely occupied.

Matt couldn't finish dinner fast enough. The food was excellent, he had to give it that. But he could hear the chatter behind him between the innkeeper and her child. Their laughter sparked memories of happier times—when he and his small family had shared meals together. Etienne would have been seven now. The pain that gripped his heart squeezed again. His adored son, now buried beside his mother in the family plot. He gazed ahead for a moment, trying to blank the memories. Marabelle had scolded their son if he played around too much when out in public. Now he wished they'd let the child do whatever he wanted. He'd lived too short a time.

Madame Rousseau's son was just the age his had been when the drunk driver of the huge truck had plowed into their family sedan and instantly killed them both. He couldn't help thinking his reflexes might have been faster than hers, to escape the crash. Or if he'd been in the car, he would have died with them, and not been left behind with all the pain.

He wanted to tell the innkeeper to cherish her son. But of course he never would. He kept the pain bottled up inside and to the outside world presented a facade belying the constant anguish he lived with. Time heals all wounds, he'd been told over and over. Everyone lied. This wound didn't heal.

Only the challenges of climbing temporarily swept the memories away. Intense concentration was necessary to pit his strength against the walls of rock. And the energy expended ensured he slept most nights without nightmares.

He hoped he hadn't made a mistake in staying at the inn. He hadn't expected a young and pretty innkeeper— or a child.

As he ate he wondered about the widow behind him. Her husband had died from a climbing fall. Yet she ran a successful inn in the shadows of some spectacular day climbs. He was curious about her. His cousins would be delighted to learn that he could wonder about something and not be locked into the past. His uncle would see it as moving on. His aunt might even hold out stronger hopes.

Not that he foresaw much interaction between Madame Rousseau and him except as it concerned his stay.

Climbing was dangerous. He knew as well as the next man, a cliff, a mountain could turn rogue and the one scaling its face could end up injured or dead. Yet the challenge wouldn't let go. To climb a sheer cliff, to scale a mountain too steep and rugged for the average trekker was a challenge not to be missed. The exalta-tion when conquering each one was a high he had once relished. Man against nature. Sometimes nature won. So far in his pursuits, he'd triumphed. Not that he took joy now; it was just something to do to take his mind off his loss.

He didn't envy the pretty innkeeper. She'd have her hands full raising a son without a father. He knew Marabelle would have had lots of family to rally around if he had been the one to die. His family tried to help out, but he didn't need them. It was easier dealing with everything on his own. It was his own private hell, and he wouldn't be leaving it anytime soon.

Matt heard the commotion behind him as the bill was paid. A moment later the small boy startled him, coming to stand at his side. "Did you like dinner? Isn't this a good place to eat?" he asked, smiling up at Matt. The boy's sunny disposition penetrated his own dark thoughts.

He took in the earnest expression on the child's face and nodded. "It is a very good place to eat."

His reward was another sunny smile the child bestowed. "I like it lots," he said.

"Come along, Alexandre," his mother summoned him.

When Matt followed a few moments later, he spotted the mother and son on the beach. They had removed their shoes and obviously were going to walk back to the inn along the shore.

He hadn't walked along any beach in a long time. He watched them until others exited the restaurant, laughing, reminding him he was standing in the middle of the sidewalk. Giving into impulse, he stepped onto the beach and headed to the packed sand near the water.

The little boy danced at the edge of the sea, running almost to the water, then dancing back when the small wavelets splashed on his feet. His laughter was carefree. How long had it been since he had felt that carefree? Matt wondered. Would he ever again?

CHAPTER TWO

THE NEXT MORNING Jeanne-Marie placed the coffee press in front of the older couple from Nantes. They were both engrossed in their daily newspaper and didn't even glance up. Surveying the small dining area, she was pleased to see her guests enjoying the breakfast she provided. Three couples had requested the box lunch she also supplied to guests. Many liked to enjoy the water sports and didn't want to have to change to eat lunch at one of the establishments in town.

Breakfast, however, was the only hot meal she provided.

Mentally checking off her list, she realized Matthieu Sommer had not yet come down. Or had he left before everyone else while she was in the kitchen preparing the meal? Glancing at her watch, she noted it was almost nine. Surely he would be up and about before now.

Checking to make sure no one needed anything, she slipped back into the kitchen to begin cleaning up. Alexandre sat at the small table at the nook she reserved for their meals. He was playing with his ever-present cars and totally engrossed in his own world. Jeanne-Marie sometimes wished she could go back to being the little girl who had had no thoughts of the future, but had been happy and content in her own safe family life. Her parents were professors at the university in Berkeley, California. She missed the activities of the college town.

She missed her family more and more, but never let them know that when they called. E-mails were easier; she could get the words just right before sending. Truly she was content in St. Bart for the most part. One day she and Alexandre would go to California for a long vacation, but so far it had seemed easier for her parents to come to France than for her to take a small child so far.

She loved France. As she had loved Phillipe. This inn had come to him when his grandfather died. It was a connection she didn't want to sever. Sometimes she dreamed of what their life could have been had he not been killed. That was not to be, and those dreams had come less frequently.

Meantime, once her guests finished eating, she had dishes to clean and preparations for tomorrow's breakfast to start. She baked her own rolls and breads. She liked to prepare a quiche every couple of days, and some of the more English-styled breakfasts for those who wanted them, experimenting with different soufflés and egg dishes.

As she washed the plates and cups sometime later, Jeanne-Marie's thoughts centered on Matthieu Sommer again! She wondered what he'd done upon his return to the inn last night. He'd gone directly to his room. She did not have televisions or radios. She had a small bookcase of mysteries and romance novels, but couldn't see Matthieu Sommer sitting still to read a book. There was a restless energy about him that demanded physical outlets, not quiet reading pursuits.

Had he left early for a climb? Or had something

happened and he had become sick and was still in bed? Maybe she'd run up to check room six. Just in case.

She knew she was being foolish, but it wouldn't hurt. If he had already left, he'd never know she had checked.

At ten o'clock, Jeanne-Marie went to the front desk to work on some of the accounts. Alexandre was content to play with his toys on the veranda, clearly visible through the open French doors. The day was beautiful, balmy breezes came from the sea, the sun had not yet reached its zenith, so the temperatures were still pleasant. She spotted the envelope immediately, and recognized the bold handwriting with her name clearly written across it. Had she seen it earlier, it would have stopped her concern. And the trip to peep into room six.

She took out the sheet of paper, suddenly feeling more alive and alert than before. She quickly read the brief missive. "Wanted a full day of climbing. In case I'm not back by dark, I'm starting on Le Casse-cou climb."

She shook her head and refolded the paper. Just like him to start with the Daredevil climb. No easy warm-ups for him. At least he was smart enough to let someone know where to start looking for him if he didn't return. She shivered, thrusting away all images of what could happen to a solo climber on the face of the cliffs. There would be others around. He might find a group of two or three to join with, each climbing at his or her own rate, yet within yelling distance in case anyone got into trouble.

She tried to imagine putting her life at risk for something as nonessential as climbing. Granted, she could understand challenging oneself, but her most daring adventures were diving in the shallows of the

Mediterranean. Phillipe had loved scaling all different terrains, however. Never tiring, even on climbs he'd done before. So there had to be something to recommend it. That gene had eluded her.

As her guests came and went through the day, she couldn't help growing on edge as the afternoon waned and dusk approached. Matthieu Sommer still had not returned. She prepared dinner for herself and her son. Telling Rene to let her know when Monsieur Sommer returned, Jeanne-Marie didn't fully enjoy her dinner as worry began to rise. The minutes seemed to race by. Shouldn't he have been back by now? What if he'd fallen? What would she do if the police showed up to inform her of his death and collect his things from his room? She almost groaned in remembered agony of when she'd been so notified.

She had climbers all the time staying in the inn. She'd not worried about any of them beyond the normal concern. This was getting ridiculous. He was fine! And it was nothing to her if he weren't.

"The kid at the front desk said you wanted to see me when I returned," Matt said from the doorway to the kitchen.

Jeanne-Marie looked up and caught her breath. He looked hot, tired and a wee bit sunburned. The climbing clothes he wore were dirty and scuffed. He had a small cut on one cheek that had bled and scabbed over. His hair was gray with dust. His dark eyes held her gaze, intense and focused.

She felt her heart skip a beat, then race. Her worry had been for naught.

"I, uh, just wanted to make sure I knew when you returned. So I didn't call Search and Rescue," she said lamely.

"Hi," Alexandre said with his sunny smile. "You need a bath. Then do you want to walk on the beach with me?" His hopeful tone almost broke Jeanne-Marie's heart. It wasn't often he asked anything of their guests. She wished she had found a male friend who would provide a strong role model for her son. He saw his grandfather too infrequently.

"No, honey, Monsieur Sommer's tired and probably needs to eat supper."

"I am hungry," he confirmed.

She nodded. "Did you have anything to eat today?" Climbing took a lot out of a body; surely he knew enough to eat for fuel.

"Got breakfast at the bakery and they made up some sandwiches, which I ate perched on a small ledge with a view that encompassed half the Med. I'm thirsty more than hungry."

She jumped up and went to get him a glass of water, relieved he was safe, annoyed she had even noticed.

She handed him the glass and his fingers brushed against hers, sending a jolt of awareness to her very core. She backed off, wanting him out of her kitchen, out of her inn. He awoke feelings and interests best left dormant. She normally didn't mingle much with her guests. He had already trespassed by coming into the kitchen. Rene could have let her know.

"You can eat dinner here. Mama's a good cook," the five-year-old said.

Matt raised an eyebrow in Jeanne-Marie's direction, a silent question.

She wanted to tell him her inn provided two meals a day, and no one ate in the privacy of her own quarters. But looking at the angelic expression on her little boy

weakened her resolve. He asked for so little, was content
with life as they knew it. How could she refuse?

"Never mind, I'll get something in town," Matt said,
placing the glass on the counter.

"If you want to freshen up first, I'll warm up what
we're having. It's a stew that's been simmering all day.
I can have a plate for you in twenty minutes." There was
plenty—she had planned on it serving her and Alexandre
for two days. A plan easily changed for her son's sake.

"Deal. I'll be back in twenty minutes." He left without
another word.

Jeanne-Marie let out her held breath with a whoosh.
Turning, she went to the stove. The heat had been turned
off the stew, so she quickly began warming it. She had
fresh bread she'd made that morning. A salad and apple
crumble would be a nutritious meal for a man who had
expended untold energy pushing his body to the limit
scaling a sheer cliff.

And while he ate, she'd let him know it was a one-
time meal. She didn't provide dinner. She didn't want
him in her space. He'd be gone in a few days, nothing
permanent about guests who came and went.

Mostly she felt flustered. Personal customer service was important in running an inn, especially if she
wanted repeat customers, but that did not include sharing meals in her private domain. And especially with
someone who without effort seemed to turn her upside
down.

She and Alexandre had finished their meal by the
time Matt returned. His hair was still damp; the cut
on his cheek had been taped with a butterfly bandage.
Obviously he was used to minor scrapes and had come
prepared. His cheeks were slightly sunburned. But the

rest of him looked amazingly robust and healthy. Jeanne-Marie was not one to have fantasies about strangers who came to the inn. This aberration had to end!

"I can serve you on the veranda overlooking the sea," she suggested, jumping up and trying to get him out of her private space.

He glanced at their empty plates on the small table. "Since you're finished, that'll be fine with me."

"I can sit with you to keep you company," Alexandre volunteered, clutching two cars against his chest.

Carrying out the plate and utensils, she hoped other guests wouldn't ask for similar service. She worked hard enough without adding an extra meal for all guests into the mix.

She placed his dish on one of the glass tables that dotted the veranda. The sunscreens had been lowered earlier to keep the heat from the lounge. She pressed the switch to raise one to offer a better view, but kept the one directly in front of his table down to shelter it from the last rays of the sun.

"I'll get you something to drink," she said, hurrying back to the kitchen. Normally she kept Alexandre away from the guests when they were eating, but the few moments it took her to get the water wouldn't hurt.

She brought out a pitcher of water and a tall glass. She remembered how Phillipe gulped water as if he were dying of thirst when he returned from climbing.

"Do you need anything else?" she asked.

"No, this looks perfect," he said when she set the pitcher on the table. "I appreciate the water."

"I remember." She sat gingerly on a nearby chair, looking at the sea glowing golden as the sun descended. It would be dusk and then dark before long. Alexandre would go to bed and she'd be alone with her thoughts.

She debated returning to the kitchen. Maybe in a moment. Would it be rude to leave? Did he want privacy or should she act as a hostess?

"You spent a long day on the cliffs," she said.

"I got an early start, then prowled around a bit on the top. The view is stupendous. No wonder it's highly recommended." The words fit, but his tone lacked the enthusiasm she usually heard from climbers.

When he did not elaborate, she said, "The cliffs are so popular the government's concerned about pollution and eco damage. There's talk about closing them down, or limiting the number of people who have access." She glanced at him as he ate. He seemed to enjoy the food. Good. She was an excellent cook. But since her husband's death, she rarely entertained. At first she couldn't face having anyone over. She'd wanted to grieve in private. The first few months after his death, she'd kept busy by closing their flat in Marseilles and moving here and learning the guest services trade.

"I saw some trash and debris while I was climbing. And there was a pile of trash at the top," he said. "People can be thoughtless and careless. Those are the ones to keep out."

She nodded. "Yet how to do that? Ask if someone is thoughtless before permitting them to climb? Who would admit to it?"

He shrugged. "It'd be a shame to close access because of the acts of a few."

"If you eat all your dinner, there's apple crumble for dessert, with ice cream," Alexandre said, leaning against the table and watching as Matt ate. He'd scarcely taken his gaze off the man.

"This is a very good dinner," he told the boy.

"I helped make the bread," he said proudly. "Mama lets me punch it."

"You did an excellent job."

Alexandre smiled again and stared at Matt with open admiration.

"Did you climb a mountain today?" he asked.

"A cliff, not a mountain," Matt replied.

"My dad climbed mountains. I will, too, when I get big. I'll go to the top and see everything!"

"The views from the top are incomparable," Matt agreed.

"Can I go climbing with you? Can we go to a mountain?"

"No. Don't be pestering our guest," Jeanne-Marie said sharply. She didn't like talk about Alexandre's climbing. Too often his grand-père encouraged him by telling him all about climbs he'd done with Phillipe. She didn't think she'd ever like the thought, but realized Alexandre would be his own person when he grew up. If he took up the same hobby as his father, she hoped he wouldn't come to the same end. It scared her just thinking about it.

"He's not pestering me. Actually, I had already taken my son on a couple of easy rock climbs by the time he was Alexandre's age."

"I could go. I'm big now. I'm five." He looked at Matt with a mixture of admiration and entreaty.

Jeanne-Marie felt her heart drop. He had a son. All the more reason to remember he was merely a guest and she the hostess of the inn. And to stay away.

Jeanne-Marie didn't like that look on Alexandre's face. He'd better not get a hero fixation on this guest. Matt was only here another six days. Once before, a year or so ago, Alexandre had latched onto a guest who had been staying at the inn with his wife and daughter and who had kindly included her son in some of their activities. Alexandre had moped around for weeks after their departure, not truly understanding why they didn't come back.

"Alexandre, do you want to help me dish up the dessert?" she asked, standing quickly, anxious to put some distance between her son and guest. He wasn't exactly Mr. Congeniality. She didn't want Alexandre to pester him until he snapped something out that would hurt her son's feelings. Though if he had a son, he was probably used to little boys.

"Sure. We waited for you," he said, placing his cars on the table and running into the house.

Jeanne-Marie hoped Matt wouldn't think she had deliberately waited to be included when he ate the dessert. He was obviously married and with a child. Where was his family? Had they stayed home since he wanted serious climbing, beyond the level of a child? Had they made other plans, separate vacations? She couldn't imagine it, but some couples liked that.

Matt watched as Jeanne-Marie followed her son at a more sedate pace—but not by much. He thought of her that way, seeing her name on the brochure for the inn. He had trouble picturing her as Madame Rousseau.

She certainly hadn't had to feed him; he knew the inn didn't offer dinners. Maybe tomorrow he'd make a later start and sample both the breakfast and box lunch she offered.

Taking another deep drink of water, he watched the brush of the Mediterranean against the white sandy beach. He couldn't believe he'd mentioned his son so casually. The world hadn't ended. The searing pain had not sliced. Instead a kind of peace descended. His son had been so proud climbing the small hills they'd scrambled up together. He could remember his boasting to his mother.

He finished the simple meal and leaned back in his chair. For the first time in ages he felt almost content. He was pleasantly tired from the climb and replete with the excellent stew. And he had liked speaking of Etienne. He never wanted himself or anyone to forget his boy.

His cell phone rang. He glanced at the number and flipped it open to respond.

"Hey, man," his friend Paul said.

"What's up?" Matt responded. He knew—Paul was partying already. He could hear the background noise of a club.

"Having a great time. You should come over. It wouldn't be that long a drive, would it? I've got some hot babes lined up. We can party until dawn."

Over the last year Paul had tried to set him up with several women. His friend felt enough time had passed for Matt to get back into the dating scene. Never having married himself, Paul really didn't understand. There was no magical time to stop grieving. No magical moment when a man said forget the past, marry again. Matt couldn't see himself deliberately putting his heart and emotions at risk. Once shattered, he wasn't willing to take the risk of getting involved again. The fear of another marriage ending suddenly and horribly couldn't be ignored. He'd had his shot at happiness. Now it was time to come to terms with the hand life had dealt.

"Party until dawn and then go climbing?" Matt asked. A sure formula for disaster.

"We could sleep in a little, then hit the cliffs. I got

in a climb today. Beat my own record for going up and back," Paul said.

Even in climbing Paul couldn't lose his competitiveness.

"Did you like the view?" Matt asked.

"What view? Water below me, rock in my face. Hey, I could show you that climb tomorrow, race you to the top."

Jeanne-Marie and her son stepped out onto the veranda, three bowls on a tray. Alexandre proudly carried spoons.

Another time Matt might have skipped dessert, but he was tempted by the novelty of eating with her and her son. Now it also provided a good excuse to end the call.

"You have a drink for me, Paul. I'll skip tonight but be in touch. We'll meet up later in the week and scale something together."

"Ah, man, you'll be missing some kind of fun."

"My loss," Matt said, not believing a word. He flipped the phone closed as Jeanne-Marie placed one of the bowls in front of him. Alexandre solemnly handed him a spoon, then scampered around to sit in the chair across from him. Jeanne-Marie placed a bowl with a smaller serving in front of Alexandre. Jeanne-Marie sat to Matt's right, throwing him an uncertain look as if not sure of her welcome.

He was momentarily taken aback. Giving in with poor grace, he accepted they would sit with him until each had finished their dessert.

The apple crumble was warm and cinnamony, the rich vanilla ice cream a delicious addition. The dessert almost melted in his mouth.

"This is delicious." Even his own cook rarely had a dessert as tasty as this.

"Thank you."

"You should offer dinner to your guests. They'd enjoy your cooking." He had enjoyed it. And the fact he didn't have to leave the inn.

She smiled shyly and shook her head. "I have everything going the way I like. There's such a thing as too much, you know."

"Such as?"

"Trading my afternoons with Alexandre to cook for as many as fifteen people day in, day out would be too much. I try to be creative with my breakfasts, though. You'd know if you try them."

"I plan to sample one in the morning. If I can still get an early start."

"I can provide breakfast as early as six-thirty if I know ahead of time. Sometimes people go diving or out on one of the cruise ships and need an equally early start. I also fix the box lunches for them to take."

"Six-thirty it is."

Matt savored the dessert. He watched Alexandre scrape every bit of it from his bowl and lick his spoon as if hoping more would appear. It reminded him of Etienne. He almost smiled, then felt a pang at his loss. Was that a trait of all little boys? Etienne would have loved this dessert.

Alexandre looked up at Matt, dropping his spoon in the bowl with a clatter. "Can you go for a walk with me now? And can you take me to climb a mountain?"

"Monsieur Sommer is too tired to go walking with us," Jeanne-Marie said quickly. "And there are no mountains nearby."

Truth was he would relish an early night, but the

look of disappointment on the boy's face and the quick way she'd tried to shut him out perversely caused him to agree to the walk. He wasn't sure why he wanted to spend more time with them, but the less she wanted him around, the more he wanted to stay. There was nothing in his room but memories he'd just as soon forget.

"I'm not eighty. A good meal and I'm ready to go. A short walk sounds like just the thing before bed," he said, holding her gaze for a moment in challenge.

"It becomes rocky the closer to Les Calanques we go," she said, glancing at the cliffs, now growing dark and mysterious as the last of the daylight faded.

What was it about her that made him want to spend time with her? Normally he stayed away from people. Was it the novelty of someone not tiptoeing around him that had him interested? Or her quiet appeal that he found intriguing? She didn't flirt, didn't try to sound witty and entertaining. Didn't avoid subjects for fear of his reaction. Of course, she didn't know about his wife and child. That might change matters.

Jeanne-Marie cleared their bowls and spoke to Rene before returning to the veranda. Matt listened to Alexandre talking about his day playing with his race cars and how he helped make the bread and that he still had to take naps, which he didn't need anymore because he wasn't a baby and would be starting kindergarten in the fall. And about how his dad had climbed very high mountains and he wanted to as well.

Matt nodded at Alexandre's earnest conversation and remembered Etienne had been like that. He remembered his son going on and on like this boy did. And he remembered his following Matt around the vineyard, questioning everything. He had had a million questions. God, Matt wished he'd been able to answer them all.

"A short walk," Jeanne-Marie said when she returned onto the veranda.

When Matt stood, Alexandre slipped his small hand in his larger one. He was startled by the feeling of protectiveness that surged toward this small boy. He missed his son. He'd had him until his fifth year. Not nearly long enough. Etienne should have grown up, married, lived a full life.

Instead he was gone.

But for a few moments, Matt would suspend the past and just be with a small boy. And remember the happier days with his own son.

The walk along the beach would have been in silence except for the constant babble from Alexandre. He seemed capable of chattering away forever without comment from either adult. Not that Matt had anything to say. The sea on one side, the last of the establishments on the other and the cliffs ahead. It didn't call for much comment.

Jeanne-Marie looked at him, her expression bemused. "You're doing well with this. I guess it comes from being around your own son. He can talk your ear off."

"He's young, still learning so much. Life is easier at that age." Oddly he was enjoying the walk. It was amazing what a five-year-old had to talk about. The poignant loss of his son was overshadowed by the delight this child had in his surroundings.

"Did you grow up here?" he asked when Alexandre pulled away to run ahead to a piece of driftwood.

She shook her head. It was harder to see her as the light waned. Soon they'd have to be guided by the lights spilling out from the scattered buildings along the beach.

"I was born and raised in California. My parents

are both professors at the university in Berkeley. We lived not too far from the campus. I met Phillipe when I came to France as an exchange student in my junior year. I stayed and graduated from La Sorbonne. When we married, we lived in Marseilles. That's where he was from. His parents still live there."

"So you chose this inn rather than return to America?"

"Phillipe's grandfather left it to him. We had a manager running it when he was alive. But we spent a lot of time here when he wasn't working. After his death, I thought this would keep me closer somehow. Plus it gives me the opportunity to make a living and still be able to spend most of the day with my son. And keep him near enough to see his grandparents. Alexandre's all they have left of their only child."

"It's a charming village. But quiet."

"True. It suits us at this stage in our lives."

He wished he could see her expression. "What do you do in the evenings?"

"Read. Work on the accounts if I don't get a chance during the day. I have a computer and keep in touch with my family and friends. And I have Alexandre."

"He can't be much of a conversationalist, though you wouldn't know it by his chatter tonight. It's captivating, actually."

She smiled, barely visible in the dim light. "He can be funny and wise at the same time—and all without knowing it. I'm content with my life. Why would I change it?"

"To find another husband. It can't be easy to be a single parent."

"I had one. I don't expect a second."

"Men aren't rationed, one per woman."

She shrugged. "How many wives have you had?" she asked.

He paused a second before replying, "One."

"Ah, the contented married man," she said.

"A drunk driver killed her and our son. Two years ago now."

"I'm sorry. How horrible." Jeanne-Marie was stunned. She couldn't imagine losing both Phillipe and Alexandre. Sympathetically she reached out to touch his arm. "I'm so sorry for your loss."

They walked in silence for a moment, then hoping she wasn't making things worse, she asked, "Where do you live?"

"Family enterprise in the Vallée de la Loire."

"Castles and vineyards," she murmured. "Do you have a castle?" she asked whimsically.

He paused a moment. She wished the light was better so she could see his expression.

"My family has one," he finally said.

"You're kidding! How astonishing. Are those old castles as hard to heat as they look?"

Matt was surprised by her question. Most of the time if the castle came into discussion—which he tried to avoid—the first question was how large was it and when could the person see it. "The rooms we don't use are closed off, and those in use comprise the size of a normal house, so it's not as hard to heat as you might suspect."

"Sorry, it's none of my business, but every time I've seen one, I've wondered how in the world it's heated. We don't have such a problem in winter here with the warmer climate."

"Are you a king?" Alexandre asked.

"No. The castle has been in the family for many

generations. But I work for a living like anyone else," Matt said.

"At the family enterprise?" she asked.

"Vineyards and a winery." There. Now see what the woman did with that knowledge.

"Mon Dieu, vin de Sommer—I've heard about your wines. They're excellent." She stopped abruptly and looked at him. He stopped and looked at her. The stars did not shed much illumination, so he couldn't see her expression well.

"Are you telling me the truth?" she asked, trying to see him clearly.

"I don't lie," he said calmly. What, did she think he was trying to puff himself up? To what end? He was here for escape, nothing more. He certainly was not out to impress her or anyone else.

"Then why are you at my inn instead of a five-star place in another town?"

"I want what you're offering—peace, quiet and an excellent vantage point to scale Les Calanques." Not the nightlife Paul loved. That he and Marabelle had once loved.

The fact his innkeeper piqued his curiosity was a turn he had not expected. It had been twenty-four months, two weeks and four days since he'd found his interest captivated by anything.

Now that she knew who he was, how long before she changed her attitude toward him? He wished he'd kept his mouth shut! No one needed to know his own tragedy. Sympathy was wasted; it didn't change anything.

"Alexandre, time for bed." Jeanne-Marie calmly took her son's hand when he ran over and began walking toward the inn, cutting obliquely across the sand to reach it sooner than walking along the water's edge.

She didn't say another word to him as he kept pace with them. Once in the inn, she went directly back to their private quarters with only a brief word of good-night.

Matt stood in the lounge watching the closed door for several seconds after she firmly shut it. Of all the reactions he'd anticipated, that had not even been on the list.

"Do you need something, *monsieur?*" the teen behind the desk asked.

"Insight into women," he said.

"Pardon?"

"Never mind." Matt took the stairs two at a time, wondering what exactly had caused him to choose this inn. And why the innkeeper would spark an interest in an otherwise gray world.

CHAPTER THREE

JEANNE-MARIE rose early the next morning to prepare breakfast for her guests—starting with Matthieu
Sommer, millionaire extraordinaire and daredevil
climber. She knew enough about the wine business,
and the Sommer name, to know the normal circles he
traveled in were far removed from her family inn. If
there was anything further to prove that she needed to
keep her distance from this guest, learning that about
him provided it.

She'd felt vaguely sad all evening, due to learning
about his own wife and son's deaths. How horrible to
lose a wife, but even more devastating to lose his son.
She didn't know how she'd go on if something happened
to Alexandre. Poor man. Truly all the money in the
world couldn't bring back a loved one.

The fresh warm croissants waited in a basket, and
she pulled the *pain de raisin* from the oven, taking in
the delicious cinnamony fragrance as she turned it out
onto a cooling rack. Cooking soothed her and brought
her joy. She was glad her guests liked her offerings.

"It smells as good as the bakery in here," Matt said
from the doorway.

She looked up and frowned. "If you sit at one of the
tables in the dining area, I'll bring your breakfast out in

a moment." She'd set the tables the night before to save one step in the morning. The two tables by the windows overlooked the garden. As he was first down, he'd have his choice of places in the dining area.

"This is fine." He crossed the floor and sat at their small family table by the windows in the nook. She frowned at his presumption. This was family space. Still, it was early—maybe he didn't want to sit alone in the dining room if she was working here. She could more easily make sure he had everything he needed.

Setting a basket of assorted warm breads and croissants on the table, she asked if he preferred coffee or hot chocolate, annoyed at her rationalization.

"Chocolate. Extra sugar and energy," he said.

Jeanne-Marie brought an assortment of jams and jellies and placed them on the table. "I'll have your drink ready in a moment."

She returned to preparing more bread for her other guests, keeping an eye on the baguettes baking. Timing was not as easy with one guest eating well in advance of the others, but some of the breads would be just as good cold as hot, and she always had plenty left over to use for the box lunches.

She did her best to ignore her unwanted visitor. Normally she had the kitchen to herself. Alexandre didn't waken until eight most mornings. She loved the quiet time preparing the breakfasts and enjoying her own cup of chocolate. Today she felt self-conscious with Matt's dark eyes tracking her every move.

"The more I learn about you, the more I'm convinced you're not making the most of your talent," he said.

She flicked him a glance. "Like what?" she asked.

"Your meals are fantastic. You could make a fortune opening a restaurant."

"I told you, I like my life the way it is. It's not all about making money."

"Money is always helpful."

Stopping for a moment, she looked at him. "Money can buy things. If things are what you want. It can't buy back a lost life."

That was true. He'd give all his fortune for things to have turned out differently two years ago. Had he been driving, would his reflexes have been better than Marabelle's? Could the accident have been avoided?

She couldn't help flicking a glance his way from time to time. His eyes met hers each time. Didn't he have someplace else to look? The view wasn't as good as from the dining room window, but he could see the garden if he sat in another chair.

"So today you again risk life and limb," she commented, wanting the topic to shift from her.

"Hardly. Merely a climb." His eyes studied her speculatively.

Jeanne-Marie felt her heart skip a beat. Frowning, she turned slightly so looking up wouldn't mean she'd instantly meet his gaze.

"If you climbed to the top yesterday, you saw the view. What drives you today?"

"Today I take on a different climb."

She shrugged. "Same view from the top."

"Have you ever seen it?"

She nodded. "Sure, many times. There's an access road that winds along the top of Les Calanques. The scenery is spectacular. And that's a much safer way to see it."

"But not as challenging."

"Perhaps men and women are wired differently. I

have no desire to spend hours clinging to a sheer face of rock."

"What do you like spending hours doing?" he asked.

She looked up, smiling shyly. "I love to bake. And so I indulge myself with homemade breads and rolls and sometimes a special dessert I can serve for special occasions like *La Victoire de 1945* coming up."

The buzzer sounded. The last of the breads was finished. She lined the bread baskets with fresh linen napkins and began dishing jellies and jams into individual serving bowls to place on each table. In twenty minutes, she'd begin brewing the coffee and make sure she had lots of chocolate ready for those who wished that.

Daring to find out more about her guest, she took her own mug of hot chocolate and leaned against the kitchen island looking at him as she sipped the fragrant beverage. "Do you have family who wonders why you climb?" she asked.

"Of course I have family. And a cousin who often goes with me. Not everyone dies who climbs."

"I know that. Phillipe's father actually taught him. It was an activity they enjoyed together. But he wasn't on the K2 climb that proved fatal."

"Lots of people climb for the sheer exhilaration, not just men. And most never have a more serious mishap than scraped knuckles or at worst a broken bone," he said. He rose and carried his mug across the kitchen, ending up close enough to invade her space. For a moment she felt her breath catch and hold. She wanted to move away, but she was hemmed in and didn't want to show how nervous he made her. She was almost thirty years old, far too old to feel this way.

"I'd like the box lunch special," he said, leaning almost close enough to kiss her.

Kiss her? Where had that thought come from?

For an instant the words didn't register. Jeanne-Marie was mesmerized. She could smell his scent, fresh and clean like the forest after a rain. She saw the tiny lines radiating from the edge of his eyes, the smooth cheeks recently shaved. She could feel the leashed energy that was appealing and fascinating in the same instant. And still see that hurt in his eyes. Now she knew what caused it; she'd seen a similar pain in her own.

Suddenly aware of the seconds that had ticked by she slid a step to the side, breaking eye contact. "Of course," she said, turning to take one of the fresh baguettes from the rack. Her hands trembled slightly and her breathing still felt off. Every inch of her skin quivered with awareness. He still stood too close. He unnerved her. Made her aware of her own femininity as she hadn't felt it in years.

Quickly making a sandwich, she wrapped it. Then she assembled the cookies, apple and packaged juice, stashing them in one of her lunch boxes, with a picture of her inn and the sea wrapping around the edges. She turned and thrust it at him.

"Don't litter," she warned. "The conservationists will know exactly where it came from if you do."

"Is that the reason for the picture?" he asked, studying the box a moment, then looking at her again.

"Some people like to take the boxes home and use them for keepsakes—a reminder of their stay here. I had one couple buy a dozen empty boxes to take home to use when giving gifts to family."

"Good idea. I'll see you later." He turned and left without another word.

Jeanne-Marie felt a sudden relief. She was alone again. Quickly clearing his place and rinsing the dishes, she tried to get her mind in gear for the coming day, and erase all traces of her recent guest. But she lingered on the memory of his strong presence. She would make sure if he came tomorrow morning for breakfast to serve him in the dining room!

Matt returned to the inn earlier than the previous day. He'd climbed another ghost of a trail up a west-facing cliff with three others attempting it whom he'd met at the bottom. It was easier than yesterday's climb had been and he'd not lingered as long at the top as the previous day. The lunch Jeanne-Marie Rousseau had made caused him to think about her bustling around her kitchen that morning. He had a cook at the château, but he rarely spent any time there now that he was grown. As a child, he'd loved to invade the kitchen anytime she was making cookies.

Parking his car in the graveled lot, he grabbed his gear—including the trash from lunch which he had packed out—and headed for his room. There were three women sitting in the shade of the veranda. In the middle, Jeanne-Marie. Laughter filled the air when the ladies raised their glasses in some kind of toast. Taking a sip, Jeanne-Marie spotted him.

She spoke softly and the other two women turned to watch him walk toward the wide-open French doors. Then he spotted four children playing in the doorway, Alexandre with his cars, another little boy wearing glasses and two girls—obviously twins. A domestic scene he'd once had at his own home.

"I see you made it through another day climbing," Jeanne-Marie said. He nodded and headed inside.

Halfway up the stairs he heard Alexandre following him. Turning, he looked as the little boy raced up the stairs to join him.

"Can I go with you?" he asked, tilting his back so far Matt was afraid the boy might lose his balance and tumble down the stairs.

"I'm going to shower and change."

"When you go climbing. Can I go with you? I want to learn."

"That's something your mother has to decide."

"I'm big."

Matt nodded gravely. "I can see that."

"She can't take me. She doesn't know how. But you could."

Matt started to turn away, but the pleading look in those warm brown eyes held him. So different from Etienne's bright blue eyes, yet the same trust and faith in adults. He didn't know this child or the mother. But he could recognize yearning. "We'll ask your mother later." He expected Jeanne-Marie would refuse, so that let him off the hook.

"Okay. Do you want to go swimming with me now?" Alexandre asked. "You can change and then you can come play with me in the sand. Mama won't let me go out on the beach by myself. I need a grown-up. I want to play by the water."

"Your mother knows best," Matt said. The little boy looked so earnest. He resumed walking up the stairs.

"She would let me go with a grown-up. Can you be the grown-up? Please?"

Matt hesitated. Children required so little to make their worlds happy. What would Etienne have done had the situation been reversed and Matt had lost his life, leaving his son behind? Who would have spared some time for his son?

"I'll be good and not go into the water unless you tell me I can," Alexandre said, running up three more steps.

Matt looked at the beseeching face and considered the possibility. He'd want someone to be there for his son. A swim in the sea sounded good. He could shower afterward.

"I'll take a quick swim and then if it's okay with your mother, you can come on the sand with me," he said.

Alexandre beamed his smile and raced down the stairs to go ask his mother.

Matt continued to his room wondering if he were losing it. He was here to forget the constant pain; now he was subjecting himself to more? Seeing Alexandre play on the sand would remind him of Etienne. Yet, oddly enough, the ache he normally felt when thinking of his son was not as strong. He was convinced Etienne was in a better place. Another man's son needed some attention. How odd Alexandre had chosen him.

Matt entered his room and quickly exchanged climbing clothes for swimming attire, pulled on a T-shirt and grabbed one of the large fluffy bath towels from the rack before heading back outside. He could hear the women as he descended the stairs but they hadn't heard his bare feet on the wooden steps.

"Honestly, Jeanne-Marie, if you don't explore possibilities, I'll disown you."

"He's just a guest." Matt recognized his hostess's voice.

"If he's taking Alexandre for a swim, I'd say he was looking to make points," the second woman said.

"No, he's only a guest being polite. You know I don't socialize with my guests," Jeanne-Marie protested.

He continued walking closer, unabashedly eaves-dropping. So she didn't socialize with her guests. He wondered why. Some might demand more, like dinner in the evening, he thought. Seems as if he had been lucky she'd spent time with him last evening, even though her son was there as well.

Sidestepping around the children, Matt walked out to the veranda. Alexandre spotted him immediately and rushed over. "Mama says I'm not to bother you. I won't be a bother, will I?"

"No. I would not have agreed if I hadn't meant it," he told Jeanne-Marie. Glancing at the other two women, he saw them look first at him and then at their friend, smiles showing.

Feeling like he was on some kind of stage, he walked out to the sand and to the water's edge. He wished he'd heard more about Jeanne-Marie. What was she to do lest her friend disown her?

He pulled off the T-shirt, dropping it and his towel near the water, and plunged into the sea, trying to drive away the thoughts that were coming to mind. He had been happily married. Then torn by tragedy. Less in-volvement in everything would keep further pain at bay. He went to work, avoiding the long evening walks in the vineyards that reminded him of the times Marabelle and Etienne had accompanied him.

He dutifully checked in with his aunt and uncle and cousins. More to keep them from driving over to check in on him than because he wanted to keep in contact. It was easier to cocoon himself in work and ignore the rest. He would not willingly give his heart as hostage to fate again.

The water was cool and buoyant. He swam some distance from the shore. When he paused to tread water, he studied the village from his vantage point. Fishing boats bobbed in the marina to his far right. There were several establishments that had patios dotted with tables facing the sea, with tourists enjoying the afternoon sun.

It was good to swim after the climb. Later he'd eat in the village and see what activities were planned for *La Fête de la Victoire de 1945* this weekend. He expected the small village to celebrate in a big way. Not that he planned to celebrate. He remembered—then banished the memory from his mind. He would not think of other fetes and how he and his family had celebrated. The year before last had been the worst. The first of every holiday without Marabelle and Etienne had been the hardest, at least that's what everyone told him when he'd growled like a bear in pain if anyone in the family wished him happy. He felt all holidays proved hard now.

Refreshed by his swim, Matt headed for the shore. He had no sooner stepped from the water than Alexandre raced across the sand to join him. Toweling off, he was touched by the child's trust and desire to spend time with him. His cousin candidly told him he was a bear to be around.

If anyone had told him a week ago that he'd be entertained by a small boy at the side of the sea, he'd have called the person crazy. But sitting beside Alexandre listening to him talk was as enjoyable as anything he'd done lately. The child didn't need encouragement; his running monologue continued with only an occasional hmm from Matt.

The self-imposed exile from all things familiar meant he had more time to think than he normally had. Spending time with Alexandre kept thoughts away—except about the child's mother. He looked back, but the women were gone from the veranda. It surprised him she trusted a stranger with her son. Then she stepped out and looked toward them, waving once. So she was keeping an eye on them.

Matt turned back to face the sea. This was a one-off deal. Tomorrow he'd make sure not to return to the inn until too late to be beguiled by a little boy.

"About ready to head back?" Matt asked the boy as the afternoon waned. A quick shower and he'd be back downstairs seeking a good restaurant for dinner.

"Do we have to?" Alexandre asked, looking up at Matt. "This is fun."

"I need to shower and get ready for dinner," he said, pulling his T-shirt back on. He wanted to rinse off the salt water and get into clean clothes. Standing, he looked out at the sea. This trip had been a good idea. While he'd hoped the intense concentration required for climbing would cause his focus to change, being with this boy surprisingly also helped. How unexpected!

Alexandre rose and trotted along beside Matt as they headed back to the inn. When they drew closer, Matt saw Jeanne-Marie with an older couple on the veranda. The woman had brown hair and wore expensive slacks. The older man was dressed casually.

Alexandre stopped when he saw them and grinned. "It's my grand-mère and grand-père! Come on." He began running toward the veranda.

Jeanne-Marie glanced over her mother-in-law's shoulder and saw Matt walking toward them, Alexandre racing ahead. The unexpected arrival of Adrienne and Antoine Rousseau surprised her. They hadn't called, just driven over from Marseilles. Her son had seen them and was running to greet them. Every time she saw them together reaffirmed the wisdom of her staying in France even when her parents urged her to return home.

Adrienne saw her glance for she turned. Spotting Alexandre she smiled, then faltered when she saw a stranger.

"Who's that man?" she asked.

Antoine turned, frowning.

Jeanne-Marie waited a moment until the two were closer. "This is one of my guests, Matthieu Sommer. He graciously agreed to watch Alexandre play by the water."

"Hi," Alexandre said, reaching the older couple. Both reached out to hug him.

By the time Matt stepped on the cool tiles of the veranda, he was close enough for introductions.

"Matthieu Sommer, my in-laws, Adrienne and Antoine Rousseau."

Antoine offered his hand.

Matt shook it, greeted Madame Rousseau and then headed into the inn.

Jeanne-Marie knew she would be questioned by Adrienne. Turning, she smiled brightly.

"Would you like to stay for dinner?" she asked.

"I'll take us all out to dinner," Antoine said, "so you don't have to cook. We wanted to talk about summer plans. We hope Alexandre can come visit sometimes, and give you a break."

"The summer months are always so busy. I remember from when I was a girl and lived here," Adrienne said.

"I'll clean up Alexandre and we'd be delighted to join you. Perhaps you'd like a glass of lemonade while you wait?"

"We'll be fine. We'll sit here on the veranda. Hurry,

Alexandre," Adrienne said. "We want to hear all about
what you've been doing."

He grinned and raced into the lounge. Jeanne-Marie
caught up with him when they entered their private
quarters.

"Can Matt eat with us?" he asked when she took him
into the bathroom to give him a quick wash.

"We don't eat with guests as a rule," she murmured.
She hoped he wouldn't mention the meal she'd given
Matt last night. She also hoped Adrienne and Antoine
didn't read more into Matt's watching Alexandre than
was there. There was nothing to talk about, and she
didn't want her in-laws to get the wrong impression.

Forty minutes later Jeanne-Marie and the Rousseaus
entered the town's most elegant restaurant, Les Trois
Filles en Pierre. They were soon seated at a round table
with a view of the sea. When Jeanne-Marie looked
up from her menu, her gaze was caught by Matthieu
Sommer sitting directly in her line of sight. She blinked.
How had he chosen the same restaurant as they? And
beat them here to boot?

"There's Matt. Can he eat with us?" Alexandre asked,
waving at the man. "He's my friend. He'll be lonely
eating by himself."

"I'm sure he can manage," Antoine said, studying
the menu. He glanced up at Jeanne-Marie. "Unless you
think he should join us for some reason."

She shook her head. "He's a guest at the inn, nothing
more." Good heavens, she did not want her in-laws to
think she was seeing the man.

She frowned and bent her head as if she were studying the menu. What would they think if she ever did
become interested in another man? It didn't mean she
loved Phillipe any less. Still, in all likelihood, they'd

feel threatened that someone else was trying to take their son's place.

"Ready to order?" Antoine asked.

She focused on the listings and blotted out all thoughts of falling for anyone. It was unlikely. She thought she was over Phillipe's death, but to make a life with some-one else would be too strange.

"Why can't Matt eat with us?" Alexandre asked.

"Really, Alexandre. The man's a paying guest at your mother's establishment. Not a friend," Adrienne said, scolding.

"He is, too, my friend, isn't he, Mama?"

"An acquaintance, at least," Jeanne-Marie said. "But your grandparents want to spend the dinner with you and me, not someone they don't know."

Alexandre got a mulish look to his face and slumped down in his chair, kicking his foot against one of the legs.

"Sit up, Alexandre," Antoine ordered sharply.

"I don't have to," he replied, not looking at his grandfather.

Not wanting to cause a scene, Jeanne-Marie leaned over and spoke softly into Alexandre's ear. After only a moment, he sat up and smiled at his mother. "I'll be the bestest boy in the restaurant!"

Adrienne narrowed her eyes. "What did you tell him?"

"That he's to behave. He'll be fine. I believe I'll have the pasta Alfredo," she said calmly, refusing to admit to bribing him to get good behavior. She wasn't sure how his grandparents would view her tactics. Or even if she could bring about the promised treat if he was good.

She hoped Alexandre didn't give away the secret that she'd said he could ask to walk home with Matt Sommer and not ride back with his grandparents. She hoped she could catch Matt before he left and implore his help. There was no reason for him to do so, but he'd had a son. Maybe he'd take pity on her dilemma and make Alexandre's day.

By the time Jeanne-Marie noticed Matt had called for his bill, she was growing more and more annoyed at her in-laws. They had spent the entire meal trying to talk her into letting Alexandre come for an extended visit and discussing options as if he were not sitting right there watching them with growing dismay. She smiled at him, trying to reassure him with her look, without challenging his grandparents over the meal. She knew they meant well, but he was too young to spend the entire summer away from her.

Feeling a moment of panic at the thought of Matt leaving without her even asking her favor, she jumped up. Both Antoine and Adrienne stared at her in startled surprise.

"Sorry. I'll be right back." She wound her way through the tables and reached the door just as Matthieu Sommer did.

"*Monsieur,* please, I need a huge favor. I'd so appreciate it if you'd walk back to the inn with Alexandre along the beach. I told him I'd ask if he could walk back with you if he behaved during dinner. He ended up acting like an angel. Would you please do that for me? I'll be coming as soon as we settle the bill." She was afraid to turn around, to turn her eyes anywhere but on his.

He looked beyond her at the table she just left.

"You trust your son to me?" he asked softly.

"Aren't you going back to the inn?"

He nodded.

"Then if you wouldn't mind too much, I'd be in your debt."

He looked thoughtful. "Very well. We'll walk along the beach."

"I really appreciate this. I know it's a lot to ask, but he's really taken to you."

"Then perhaps I can ask a favor in return," he said.

"Yes."

He almost smiled. "You haven't heard it yet."

"Anything. I appreciate your help."

"Early breakfast in the morning. I'd like to try another trail that's farther away from St. Bartholomeus, so I want to get an early start."

"That's no problem. I'll be home as soon as I can get there. Once you reach the inn, Rene at the front desk can watch him."

The Rousseaus looked curiously at Jeanne-Marie when she returned to the table. Alexandre looked hopeful.

"Are we leaving?" he asked, looking beyond his mother at Matt.

"After you bid your grandparents good-night," she said.

"Goodbye," Alexandre said with enthusiasm, jumping from the table and giving them each a quick hug. Then he raced across the restaurant and smiled up at Matt with trusting eyes.

"I'm ready," he said.

"So I see." Matt took the boy's hand in his and nodded toward Jeanne-Marie. Then the two of them left the restaurant.

"Whatever is going on?" Adrienne said, annoyance evident. "Why is Alexandre going off with him? Are you seeing that man?"

"No. I told you he's a guest at the hotel. He agreed to walk Alexandre back home," Jeanne-Marie said, resuming her seat. "This gives us some time to talk about Alexandre without him being around. I appreciate your wanting him to visit this summer, and I do think he'd love it. But short visits spaced over the summer, I think."

"You don't even know that man. How can you let Alexandre go off with him? He could kidnap him and we'd never see him again," Adrienne said with concern.

"I have his home address and I doubt he's planning to kidnap my son. He watched him this afternoon by the sea. He lost his own son two years ago. I think being with Alexandre reminds him of his son."

"Alexandre might not understand the attention of a stranger. He could hope for more from a guest passing through," Adrienne said quietly.

"He's used to the transient nature of our guests. It won't hurt him to spend some time with people from different areas."

"He needs a father," Adrienne said sadly.

"He had a father, a wonderful man," Jeanne-Marie said softly.

"Have him come visit us soon. We love having him," Antoine said. "And if not for the entire summer, then for as long as you can let him."

"He'd like that," Jeanne-Marie said. She wanted to get back to the inn. It wasn't that she didn't trust Matthieu Sommer. She did. But she also felt she'd imposed upon him to placate her son.

She refused a lift back to the inn, saying she wanted the walk after dinner. Once she said goodbye to her in-laws, Jeanne-Marie was grateful for the few moments alone as she hurried back home. She'd have to arrange for Alexandre to visit, but right now she was more concerned with how the walk back had gone.

When she reached the inn, she was surprised to see both Matthieu Sommer and her son sitting in chairs on the veranda in the darkness—out of the light spilling from the open French doors.

"Are you solving the world's problems?" she asked, taking one of the chairs nearby. She looked at him, then her son. She was pleased Matt had not gone directly to his room.

"Did you know Matt has horses, Mama? He rides almost every day when he's at home."

"I didn't know that. How amazing." She gave him a look of gratitude.

"Can we go visit? Then I could ride a horse," Alexandre said.

"Oh, no, honey. We live here. Monsieur Sommer is our guest. We're not his."

"I'd like to ride a horse, Mama," Alexandre persisted.

"Maybe we'll find a horse to go riding one day when you're older."

Alexandre thought about it a moment, his face scrunched up. Then he brightened and gave a brilliant smile to the man next to him. "It's later. Now can we ask Mama?"

"Ask me what?" Jeanne-Marie asked.

"Can I go climbing? He can show me how."

Jeanne-Marie frowned. "Monsieur Sommer is here to do serious climbing, not spend time teaching you how to climb."

Matt shrugged. "One afternoon wouldn't hurt. If you'd allow it. There're some very easy climbs he could probably handle. I know what a small boy can do. My son loved it."

Jeanne-Marie looked between the man and the boy. She could see the hope dancing in Alexandre's eyes.

"Mmm, we'll see. Now it's time for bed. We'll discuss climbing another time." She rose and held out her hand. The little boy slid off the chair and reached for her, looking earnestly at their guest.

"We can talk more tomorrow."

"Perhaps." Jeanne-Marie did not want her son pestering the guests. Even though Matt had been kind enough to escort her son home, she was not in the habit of imposing on people at the inn.

After Alexandre was in bed, Jeanne-Marie caught up on some household chores, then went to sit on the veranda. It was nice to relax in the darkness and wait for the last of her guests to return for the night. Sometimes she almost could imagine she was waiting for Phillipe to return from a walk.

Though tonight her thoughts were of Matthieu Sommer. She wished he wanted a last bit of fresh air and would join her on the veranda.

The evening was cool. Settling in the shadows, she gazed toward the sea, dark and mysterious this late. Reviewing her in-laws' visit, she wished they'd spoken about Phillipe more. She missed him. Missed all the family traditions they'd just begun. Like *La Victoire de 1945*. Last year she and Alexandre had gone with her friend Michelle and her family. Alexandre had enjoyed the activities, but she'd felt out of place every time Michelle's husband had swung his son up onto his shoulders so he could see better. Alexandre should have had a father to do the same thing! He was growing so big, it was hard for her to pick him up. Not that her holding him gave him that much extra height.

The last fete she'd attended with Phillipe, Alexandre had been an infant in arms. She remembered the day with a soft smile, startled to realize that the achy pain that normally came when she remembered something done with her late husband was missing. She hoped she'd reach the stage to remember their time with nostalgia and a poignant feeling of days gone by. But for the first time she didn't feel crushed with the weight of grief. Was she at last moving on, as so many had told her she would?

Did meeting Matthieu Sommer have anything to do with that? She almost gasped at the thought.

CHAPTER FOUR

THE NEXT MORNING Jeanne-Marie was in the midst of preparing individual quiches for her guests when Matthieu Sommer walked into the kitchen. She looked up, feeling a spark of delight, which she firmly and immediately squashed.

"I can serve breakfast in the dining area," she said, finishing the last of the crusts and carefully lifting portions into the miniature pie pans she used for the individual servings. Guests usually loved her quiches; her crusts were light and flaky, the warm filling an assortment that so many seemed to enjoy.

"Here's fine," he said, sitting at the same place as yesterday.

"This is a working kitchen."

"Is there a problem?"

She frowned, wondering how to convey how self-conscious he made her without sounding like an idiot. *Please, go in the other room before I lose sense of what I'm doing and just stare at you,* wouldn't go over very well. Sighing softly, she began to make his hot chocolate. Taking the mug to the table, she placed it down in front of him. His hand reached to hold her arm. "Is there a problem?"

The tingling that coursed through her warmed deep

inside. She took a shaky breath. "I guess not. I'm not used to people being in here while I'm working."

There was a definite, huge, mega problem—she was so aware of him as a man, and her own dormant needs as a woman, she couldn't think of anything else. His hand was warm on her arm. The scent of him had her own senses roiling. She'd give anything to be brave enough to sit down with him and forget about the rest of her guests while she learned every aspect about his life she could discover.

"I'll be as quiet as a mouse," he said solemnly.

"Not a good analogy to use in a commercial kitchen," she said, reluctant to pull her arm from his gentle grasp. His thumb brushed against her skin lightly. It sent shivers up her back. With that, she turned away and scurried behind the high counter, doing her best to remember she was in charge of the inn and he was a guest who would be leaving soon. Not a man to get interested in. No someone to start a relationship with.

The thought stunned her. She'd never thought to fall in love again. She'd adored Phillipe. They'd had a wonderful marriage. Too soon over, but she'd never expected to become involved with another man.

Then, she'd never met a man who piqued her interest as much as Matthieu Sommer. Or was as different from Phillipe as he could be. Where her husband had been friendly and outgoing, easily making friends wherever he went, Matt was quiet, kept to himself and seemed to ignore the rest of the world.

"The quiche won't be ready for a half hour. I have some fresh croissants and breads," she said. "I can make you an omelet."

He checked his watch. "I'd planned to leave early, but my friend Paul called last night. He and I'll climb together today. I'm meeting him in Marseilles. We're tackling a cliff on that side. But he won't get up until I pound on his door, if I know him. He was probably up until after two."

Jeanne-Marie looked at him. "So why didn't you stay in Marseilles?"

"This place suits me."

"Mmm." If he'd never come, she'd never have met him. That wouldn't have been all bad. She didn't like the sensations that rose whenever he was near. It reminded her of all she'd lost. And filled her with a vague yearning for things that couldn't be.

Matt watched Jeanne-Marie as she worked. She seemed to enjoy cooking. She could make so much more money if she expanded her meals. Not everyone was so talented or content with less than she might achieve.

Thinking about it, he realized she'd not changed her attitude toward him, either, once she'd learned about his family's situation. She still treated him as any guest, no more sympathy or less than for any other. At least she didn't tiptoe around, afraid to say anything that might remind him of his wife and son.

Jeanne-Marie was that rare individual who seemed genuinely content with life as it was. Too bad he couldn't feel the same way. The raw grief that wouldn't fade drove him. He wanted to escape his thoughts and find some change in climbing, in pushing himself to the limit. Sleep then would be uneventful and deep.

"Here you go. And I warmed a croissant for you," she said, placing in front of him a heaping plate of cheese, pepper and onion omelet, along with a fluffy croissant.

"Thank you. When do you eat breakfast?"

"Before I prepare, or I'd be nibbling all morning."

He began to eat, enjoying the flavors that burst in his mouth. After a moment, he said, "I might eat dinner in Marseilles before returning tonight."

"I won't worry then if you're late back. The center doors are left open for any guest coming in after I go to bed."

"You'd worry otherwise?" Now that was interesting.

She looked up and shrugged. "I'd worry about any guest climbing those cliffs."

He ate, finishing the delicious breakfast she'd prepared. Drinking the last of his hot chocolate, he debated asking for another cup. Instead he put it down and looked at her.

"I could take your son on an easy climb tomorrow afternoon, if you'd permit." He'd thought about it long into the night last night. Being with Alexandre was different from being with Etienne, yet on one level it was the same. Both young boys exploring their worlds. It wouldn't hurt him to spend a few hours helping in that exploration.

"Why would you do that?" she asked, studying his face as if looking for clues.

"For my son."

"Oh." She glanced away and nodded. "Then if you think Alexandre won't be a pest, I guess we could take advantage of your expertise. I don't want him to try more than he can do. But he pesters his grandfather all the time to take him climbing. Maybe trying it once or twice will have him lose interest."

"Or capture his interest even more."

"There is that risk."

"You're a good mother to let him try this when I know you don't approve."

She continued working. "It's not that I disapprove so

much as I don't want him hurt. I think all mothers feel that way. But I'm trying very hard not to be overprotective. If I had my way we'd live someplace totally flat where the most exciting thing he could think of would be to ride a bicycle."

Matt nodded. He remembered Marabelle being concerned when Etienne rode his pony. The boy had loved that pony. And he'd only fallen a couple of times. Nothing to dim the delight he took in riding.

Surprisingly, once they agreed on a time, Matt felt a spark of anticipation. Today's climb would be challenging. But tomorrow's might be more rewarding.

Much as he might like to stay for another cup of chocolate and talk to Jeanne-Marie, he had agreed to meet Paul early. He hoped his friend was ready to climb and not handicapped by a hangover.

Jeanne-Marie watched Matt leave with mixed feelings. He invaded her space, yet when he left it seemed emptier than before. She couldn't figure out how to keep him out of the kitchen. She felt disturbed by his presence. The disruption to her carefully planned life, the extra excitement of being fully alive when he was around made her restless and agitated when he left. She didn't want to come alive, to feel love and then loss. Better to stay in a state that didn't allow strong emotional feelings. It would be safer.

Shaking off her feelings, she tried to draw contentment from her baking. Her life was full, satisfying and suited her and Alexandre perfectly.

As the day progressed, Jeanne-Marie went through her normal routines. Two couples checked out. Another two were due to arrive. When her friend Michelle called to see if they were attending *La Fête de la Victoire de 1945,* Jeanne-Marie was grateful for a break.

"I'd like that. Alexandre has seen the posters I put up and has been plaguing me about when we're going."

"The parade begins at eleven. I thought we could meet at the corner where we met last year."

"Perfect. He'll be thrilled."

The celebration was a big deal in small St. Bart. Phillipe told her how often his parents had brought him to stay with his grandparents for the fete. He'd enjoyed it as a child, much as Alexandre loved it now. They'd only shared one fete here after they married. Now attending each year was special, doing something he'd done. She could tell her son about his father, and continue his memory as best she could.

Her thoughts went to Matthieu Sommer. What would he do that day, another climb? Holidays must be especially lonely for single people, she thought. And especially sad to remember them spent with loved ones now gone. The first without Phillipe had been hard—but she had Alexandre. Matt had no one.

She could invite him to join them.

She caught her breath at the thought. The last couple of years, she'd invited her guests to enjoy the fireworks from the veranda. But she'd never mingled with them during the day.

Late in the afternoon, Adrienne called.

"Antoine and I can come for Alexandre next Monday afternoon," she offered.

"I'll bring him up. I have some shopping I'd like to do in Marseilles. What time works best?"

"Of course we'd like him to come for as long as possible, so early morning, but I know you have things to do at the inn. Come when you can."

"Let's plan on early afternoon, then. Anything special going on I should make sure he has proper clothes for?"

"A swimsuit and sturdy shoes. We'll take a ramble in the park," Adrienne said.

The seaside park in Marseilles was a favorite of Alexandre's.

"He'll love that."

She hung up, happy for Alexandre to have his grandparents so near. Yet she was already missing him for when he left to visit. Usually she let him stay a few days at a time. Every so often his grandparents asked for longer, but so far Alexandre hadn't pushed for any longer visits. And she missed him too much when he was gone to agree.

She finished up her work and went to take Alexandre for a swim. He was going to be thrilled with all the plans.

It was after ten o'clock that night when Jeanne-Marie went to close up the French doors. Rene had left a half hour ago. All her guests except Matt had returned. The last couple had just gone up. How late was he planning to be? Had he decided to stay the night in Marseilles rather than drive back? If so, wouldn't he have called to let her know?

Then she heard the sound of a car on the gravel of the parking area. He was back. She couldn't help the sudden skip in her heart. Every inch of her went on alert and she waited impatiently for him to come in, holding the French door open wide.

He saw her the moment he stepped on the veranda. "I didn't keep you up, did I? I know you rise early."

"No, this is my usual closing time. Did you enjoy

climbing with your friend?" She shut the door after he walked through and turned around to face him. He was growing more tanned each day he spent on the cliffs. He had a rugged masculinity that attracted like nothing else had. She wanted to check her hair and make sure she looked as good as she could. How silly was that? Matt hadn't shown a speck of interest. He was still mourning.

"Paul's driven to competition. Everything has to be a challenge. He made bets on who would reach the top first. Then he wanted to try a different climb down. Racing to be first in both treks, he made me tired just watching him. I didn't come to make everything into a contest."

"Have you climbed together before?"

"Once or twice. I know, I should have expected it. He's always like that. Only this time, I was feeling differently about things. It's the first time I've gone with him since Marabelle and Etienne's deaths."

"Your family?" she asked gently. She hadn't known their names.

He nodded.

"Did they share your love of climbing? Your son must have, if he went with you."

"As long as it was a gentle ramble around hills and lakes. Once serious rock climbing came into the picture, Marabelle always found other pursuits. I had hoped Etienne would like to climb when he got older."

"Phillipe's father taught him. They had lots of treks together. I think it was a bonding time; they were very close."

"Any shared activity would draw parents and children closer. Etienne liked to walk around the vineyard with me. That's what I miss most, I think."

"Tell me about him. Would you like something to drink? Brandy? Coffee?"

He hesitated so long, she was sure he'd refuse. Then he nodded once and said, "I'll take a brandy if you have it."

Jeanne-Marie went back into the kitchen and drew out a bottle of fine brandy and two snifters. She carried them back to the lounge, pleased to see Matt standing near one of the comfortable sofas with a coffee table in front of it.

She set the glasses down and offered him the bottle. He poured them each a small portion of brandy and lowered himself beside her on the sofa once she sat.

"How old was Etienne?" she asked. She hoped he wanted to talk about his son. She often wanted to talk about Phillipe, to remember the good times, to share his life again with friends. It had been hard at first, but now it brought comfort.

"He was five. Alexandre's age. His hair was blond and his eyes blue. Even if he was my own, I thought he was engaging. Funny. Inquisitive."

"What was his favorite thing to do?"

"Follow me around." Matt thought for a few moments, then told her about some of the daily trips around the vineyard, or about shopping at one of the local farmers' markets. Once, he and Marabelle had lost him for a few seconds. He remembered the panic.

As he talked, Jeanne-Marie envisioned the happy family who had thought everything would go on forever. Much as she and Phillipe had done. Her heart ached at the loss of such a sweet little boy. How much more so must he feel?

Matt glanced at his watch. "It's late. I've bored you enough."

"I'm never bored hearing about children." Now or never, she thought. They'd spent almost an hour together, and her interest was as strong as ever. She could do this.

"We will be going to watch the parade for the fete on Saturday. Would you like to join us?" She held her breath.

"I don't think I'm up for celebrating." He put the empty glass on the table and rose. "I'll take off for my room now and let you get some sleep."

She stood next to him, realizing too late how close she stood. Before she could take a step back, however, he reached out and traced his finger down her cheek. "I enjoyed talking about my son. I'll always miss him. He was a part of me that I will never completely get over losing."

"I enjoyed hearing about him. I'm so sorry for your loss. I can't even imagine."

"Most people can't, I guess."

He leaned over and kissed her. For a moment it was the mere brush of lips against lips, but then he moved his hand to the back of her head and held her while his other arm reached around to draw her closer. The kiss deepened.

Jeanne-Marie was caught off guard and before she could protest or push away, he'd released her. She stared up into his eyes, afraid of the tumultuous feelings that exploded.

"Thank you," he said, and after releasing her he swiftly crossed to the stairs and took them two at a time.

She stood still, bemused, confused. "Good night," she said a moment later, feeling stunned with that kiss. She wasn't sure what to think. Had he picked up on her reaction to being around him? He had not shown any particular interest. Why a kiss?

And what a kiss. Did he do that all the time? Slowly she sat back down on the sofa still staring off toward the stairs. Her heart pounded. Licking her lips, she was still shocked. She had not seen it coming.

It had merely been a thank-you for listening. He hadn't meant anything else by it.

Matt went to the window and stared out at the night. He could still feel the imprint of Jeanne-Marie's body against his. She was not as tall as Marabelle had been. But sweet, soft, enticing. How could he have kissed her? There was nothing between them. She'd kindly listened to him talk tonight, that was all. He was lucky she hadn't slapped him silly.

He'd felt a release sharing his son, remembering their normal routines, taken for granted at the time, so precious in memories now. She understood because of her own loss and her own son. She'd shared a few funny incidents involving Alexandre, and he'd been able to counter. The time had flown by.

The room was dark, the night was dark, his thoughts were dark. How could he kiss another woman?

Yet Marabelle was gone.

She wouldn't hold it against him.

He turned and began to strip his clothes in preparation for bed. He'd never thought to kiss another woman, but there was something about Jeanne-Marie that had him momentarily forgetting who and where he was. He'd have to apologize. If she didn't kick him out of the inn first.

Lying in bed a short time later, he threw an arm over his head and clenched his fist. Instead of giving an apology, he wanted another kiss. One in which she kissed him back. How dumb could one man be?

Matt came down for breakfast later than the previous days. He was going to do some exploring around the easy marked trails and then come back for Alexandre's ramble. That is, if Jeanne-Marie would let him. There were some places where the incline was almost gentle enough to walk up. Those would be perfect for a small boy.

He came down the stairs and went to the dining room. Two tables had guests eating. One was still cluttered with dirty dishes and two others were set. He took one to the side and sat down. No sooner had he pulled out his chair than Jeanne-Marie came from the kitchen. Did she have magical powers?

"Chocolate or coffee?" she asked, coming to his table. She balanced a plastic bin on one hip.

"Coffee today." She nodded to the stack of newspapers on the buffet. "Today's papers if you care to read. I'll be right back." Swiftly she stacked the dirty dishes in the bin and carried them out of the dining room. The conversations at the other tables were quiet. He rose and took one of the daily papers from the small stack and resumed his seat.

But he wasn't really interested in the news. He leaned back in his chair and waited for Jeanne-Marie to return.

She did, with a bright smile and a carafe of hot coffee. Also on the platter was a frittata, fresh bread, orange juice and a petite cinnamon roll. She served him, then met his eyes. "Anything else?"

He could hardly ask for her to sit with him. But he missed the companionship he'd had the last couple of mornings. At least she hadn't asked him to leave. She hadn't said anything about the kiss. Were they going to ignore it?

Feeling like he'd won a reprieve, he looked at the meal. "This looks fine," he said.

"Enjoy." She checked on the other guests, then went back to the kitchen.

Alexandre came through a moment later and made a beeline for Matt.

"Hi. We're going climbing today," he said, clambering onto the chair opposite Matt. "My mama said. Are we going now?"

"This afternoon," Matt concurred gravely. "If it's still okay with your mother."

"Will we climb to the top of a mountain?"

"No, we'll start out on a small hill."

"I want to climb a mountain!"

"Climbing is a skill that has to be learned. Everyone starts out on smaller cliffs, then goes on to bigger and bigger challenges. You cannot climb a mountain at five."

Alexandre pouted for a moment. Matt hid a smile behind his coffee cup, taking a drink while the child assimilated what he'd been told. Children wanted everything immediately.

"Can I climb a mountain tomorrow?" Alexandre asked hopefully.

"You can't climb a mountain until you are as tall as I am."

The boy's eyes got big. "I'll never be that tall."

"When you grow up you will." For a moment Matt wondered how tall Alexandre would be. He felt a pang of disappointment that he would likely never know.

Alexandre kicked his foot against the chair. "Are we going soon?"

"After lunch. I have things to do this morning," Matt told him.

"Can I come?"

Matt heard the echo of Etienne's voice. He'd ask just like that. How many times had Matt said not today, when, had he known the future, he'd have taken him every single time?

"I'll be on the phone with work. Then I need to scout out our route for this afternoon. But I tell you what, if your mother approves, once I'm back, we'll start learning about climbing."

"I'll go ask her," Alexandre said, slipping off the chair and running for the kitchen.

Jeanne-Marie came out an instant later and walked right to his table.

"Is Alexandre bothering you?" she asked.

"No. I told him when I finish checking in with work and scouting the climb for later, I'd go over basics with him. He needs to learn a lot to be safe on a cliff. He's still going for a climb today, right?"

Jeanne-Marie nodded her head slowly. "As long as I can go, too."

Matt gave a curt nod. He wasn't sure he wanted two pupils, especially when he had trouble keeping his mind focused when around the pretty innkeeper. Climbing demanded a lot of concentration; he hoped he could remember that.

He met her eyes, seeing the confusion there. But she merely said, "We'll be ready after lunch."

Jeanne-Marie felt almost as excited as Alexandre when she got ready to meet Matt that afternoon. She wore long pants, the cross trainers that offered good soles and a red T-shirt—hoping it would give her courage. Butterflies danced in her stomach. She had gone on some easy scrambles with Phillipe a time or two before she'd gotten pregnant. Easy according to Phillipe—she remembered being in over her head. Maybe a person needed to begin early to master the skills.

She hoped she was doing the right thing in letting her son try this. She knew he had heard so many stories from his grandfather about the climbs he and Phillipe had done, he equated all climbing with his father. She should talk more about Phillipe's work and diffuse the focus on his hobby. His passion, as it were.

Before they left their quarters, she caught Alexandre and held his face between her hands, making him look directly at her. "Listen. You must do whatever Matt tells you, understand? He's the expert. He'll keep you safe, but you have to listen to him."

"I will listen to him," Alexandre promised solemnly.

"If not, we stop and come straight home," she finished.

"Okay. I'll listen." He went racing out of their area into the lounge.

"Matt, Mama says I have to listen to you. I will—really, really hard."

Matt was standing near the French doors. He nodded at Alexandre's comment, then looked beyond him to Jeanne-Marie. She felt the butterflies kick up a notch, but wasn't sure if it was from meeting his dark gaze or the thought of letting her son climb a cliff.

"I thought we'd drive to the trailhead," Matt said.

"Fine, you're in charge." She bid Rene goodbye. The teen had come early to be there when they left.

In no time, the three of them were walking along the rocky trail that skirted the base of Les Calanques. The sea sparkled in the sunshine. The cliffs towered over them, undulating with folds and crevices. The heat of the day reflected from the rock.

"What did you learn this morning?" Matt asked Alexandre as they walked.

The boy began repeating the words of caution and preparation Matt had told him.

"Good memory," Matt said in some surprise. The child had been listening.

Jeanne-Marie was pleased at the effort Matt had made with Alexandre. He had drilled him on the safety features. She didn't know all the ones her son repeated. Phillipe had given her very little instruction, intent more on getting on with the climb.

Was Matt taking extra care because Alexandre was so young? Or was he naturally prudent? She knew from the way Phillipe had talked that he liked taking chances. She suspected Matt got the same adrenaline high from climbing, but took a bit more care to make sure he'd return in one piece.

They reached a sloping hummock that led right to the path. Matt stopped and studied it for a moment, then looked at Jeanne-Marie.

"This is the one I thought he could do."

She nodded. The hill was steep, but not sheer by any means. There were plenty of rocks to hold on to and even some small trees growing from cracks. She could almost walk up it herself without difficulty.

"This would be perfect," she said with genuine gratitude. She wouldn't have to worry about her son on this. Or herself.

"Okay, Alexandre, now listen carefully," Matt said, stooping down to be at his level. "We'll look over the entire hill first. Decide which way we want to go. Then once we begin, we'll look ahead several holds to make sure we always have a way to go. Understand?"

The boy nodded, excitement shining in his eyes.

Matt pointed out rocky protuberances they could use, some sturdy plants, some suspect. Cracks where a foot would find purchase.

Matt rose and looked at Jeanne-Marie. "Any questions?"

"Nope, I'm good to go."

"You're climbing? I thought you just wanted to observe."

"I've been listening. I think I can master this. Maybe I'll find out what all the fuss is about. Like you said, if Alexandre and I have activities in common, we might draw closer."

"Then follow us up. I want to stay near him."

Matt had Alexandre go first. Pointing out handholds and where to put his feet, Matt never was more than a foot or two away from him. Close enough to help out if anything went wrong. Close enough to catch him if the child slipped, yet giving him enough space that Alexandre would think he was doing it all on his own.

Alexandre followed Matt's instructions, climbing up the steep incline slowly and methodically.

Jeanne-Marie waited until they were well ahead and then she began her own ascent, looking ahead like Matt had instructed. It was actually fun to be going from one rock or knob to another, almost like climbing a ladder. The rock was warm beneath her fingers, the sun hot on her head. After a few feet she felt a spark of elation. She had hated the thought of this for so long, but found it was enjoyable. Another place to stand, reach up, hold on and step up.

She might never want to go up a sheer cliff or climb

a mountain, but for a gentle scramble, this was turning out much better than she had expected.

"Mama, I'm climbing!" Alexandre called, looking over his shoulder to her.

"Pay attention, Alexandre," Matt said. "Looking around can cause a distraction. Focus on the rocks."

"Okay." He climbed some more and finally reached a wide ledge. Climbing over to sit on the flat portion, he grinned as Matt joined him. "I did it. I climbed!"

"Yes, you did a great job."

Jeanne-Marie reached the ledge, looking at the two satisfied males sitting there. "I did it, too," she said, scrambling onto the ledge. It was over a dozen feet long and at least six feet from lip to back wall. A shallow cave seemed carved out behind them. Looking up, the next stage of cliff was steeper.

She sat on the edge, letting her feet dangle. They'd come almost thirty feet. Not a huge distance, but she was grateful for the attention Matt gave her son. "This is fabulous. Look how far we can see, almost to Africa." She looked at Matt. "I can't thank you enough. I can almost see what drives climbers."

He nodded. "The more familiar you become, the more you want a bit more of a challenge."

"Maybe. But for now, this suits me perfectly. Alexandre, you did so well! You'll have to tell your grand-père. He'll be proud of you."

"Maybe he will take me climbing."

"I bet he will." She thought about how he'd lost heart after Phillipe's death. But a gentle hill like this one would be perfect for him to spend time with Alexandre.

"Now are we climbing to the top?" Alexandre asked, jumping up and looking toward the rim.

CHAPTER FIVE

"NOT TODAY. We still have to get back down, and it's harder," Matt said. "You have to feel for your toeholds, because you can't see like you can going up."

Alexandre went near the edge and looked over. Matt casually reached out his hand and took hold of the child's arm. "Not too close," he said.

Jeanne-Marie felt another wave of gratitude toward the man. He was patient and alert. She knew Alexandre was safe around him. And this climb had opened her eyes about a lot of things.

In thinking about Phillipe, she knew he'd never have been as patient. He hadn't been with her. Would he have pushed Alexandre beyond what he was capable of? Or left him behind because he wasn't as skilled? Would he have taken time to teach him?

The trip back down was harder. Matt went first, and then coached Alexandre. When Jeanne-Marie looked over to try to plan her descent, she couldn't remember the way she'd come up. It looked steeper than it had coming up. Now she wasn't sure where she could find a toehold or how to make it down without falling.

"You'll do fine. Start a little to your left," Matt called up. He and Alexandre were about fifteen feet below her and to the left. She picked out a couple of places to start and eased over the edge. Reaching down for a foothold, she felt a rock. Slowly she eased her weight on it. It held. Whooshing a breath, she held on with her hands and stretched her other foot lower, moving it back and forth, trying to find a rock.

"Try a bit lower," he called.

She found the rock.

It was slow going and her arms and legs were trembling by the time she reached the bottom. But she'd made it, thanks to Matt's prompting the entire way.

Sitting down on a nearby rock, she wrapped her arms across her chest, hoping they'd feel normal in a bit.

"Wow. It's lots harder going down," she said.

"You did fine. So did Alexandre."

"But only because you were here. I might have made it up okay, but I don't think I ever would have made it down on my own."

"Sure you would. It takes practice."

"And a lot of strength. My arms and legs feel like wet noodles."

"Oh, yeah, I forgot about that." He grinned.

Jeanne-Marie stared at him. He looked ten years younger. It was the first time she'd seen him amused and it made her heart flip over. He was gorgeous. Sadness had robbed him of joy, she knew. But today, going with them, perhaps he'd forgotten for a short time and could enjoy the moment. His eyes crinkled slightly, his teeth shone white against his tan. She could stare at him all day long!

"It was fun, Mama," Alexandre said, jumping up and down. "Can we do it again?"

"Another day. If I live through this one," she murmured.

"We'll walk back to the car and you can rest there."

"Smart move, bringing the car. I don't think I could have made it all the way home otherwise," she said, struggling to stand.

Matt offered his hand and she took it. He pulled her to her feet and gave her hand a quick squeeze. Another flip-flop of her heart. She looked away lest he think she was an idiot. Slowly she started walking to the car. This had been a special day. She had learned more about herself and about the patience some men had. Not that it changed the way she felt about Phillipe, but it did raise questions she'd never thought about. He'd been a man with foibles and drawbacks like any other. Dying young didn't confer perfection.

Saturday dawned a beautiful day. The sky was crystal clear, the temperature moderate and the light breeze steady from the sea. Jeanne-Marie felt a sense of excitement and anticipation she had not experienced in years. She tried to downplay the climb, but it was all she could think about. She shouldn't become involved with anyone, especially a guest who was only staying a couple more days. There was no future in that. But she was still struck by his kindness to her son, and his care of her on the face of the rock.

She'd put the thought of his kiss firmly away. It had been a grateful father's gesture for listening to him talk about his son. Nothing romantic about it. At least not on his part. She would not embarrass herself by making more of it than he had intended.

Today she and Alexandre would spend the day with Michelle and her family, exploring all the booths of the fete, enjoying the parade and ending up in the evening sitting on the veranda to watch the fireworks that exploded over the sea, doubling the enjoyment with the reflections on the water.

Busy in the kitchen, she hoped to finish everything including cleaning up before nine. She'd left notes for her guests saying she would only serve breakfast until eight-thirty. If they didn't come down by then, she would place a cold collection of continental breakfast rolls and biscuits and hot coffee on a serve yourself basis on the buffet.

So far everyone but the couple in room three and Matt had been served. Just as she carried a bin of used dishes toward the kitchen, Matt came down the stairs.

"I'll bring you chocolate in a moment," she said, motioning for him to take a seat at an empty table. Glad for the busy tasks facing her, she hurried to the kitchen. Dumping the plates in the sink, she placed the silverware into a soaking pan and then dried her hands. She made a new pot of hot chocolate and placed it on a tray with the hot breakfast strata, a basket of rolls and jams. Lifting it easily, she carried it out.

He'd taken a seat at one of the tables by the window. She smiled brightly and placed the edge of the tray on the table while she unloaded his breakfast. "I have strata for breakfast today. And assorted rolls and breads. Anything else I can get you?" She did not let her gaze linger. He seemed to be avoiding her eyes as well.

"This looks like all I need. Thank you." He reached for the hot chocolate. "How are you feeling today?"

She brushed her hands over her apron, trying to rein in her racing heart. A quick glance around showed everyone was eating. She wanted to escape. "The bath helped. I feel a bit stiff today, but not sore. Let me know if you need anything further," she said, tilting the tray sideways and walking back to the kitchen. She felt as if she'd run a mile.

Alexandre came running in. "Hi, Mama, is it time to go to the parade?"

"Not yet. I have to get the kitchen cleared first. Our guests are still eating."

"Is Matt there?"

"Don't bother him," Jeanne-Marie warned. She plunged into the soapy water and began washing the silverware.

When she looked up a moment later she was alone in the kitchen. Quickly drying her hands, she went to the door. Alexandre was standing beside Matt, talking earnestly.

Jeanne-Marie hurried across to them.

"Come away, Alexandre. I'll make your breakfast."

"I want to eat with Matt," he said. "Don't you want me to eat with you? If you eat alone you'll be lonely."

"He'll be fine here," Matt said.

"He can eat in the kitchen."

"He'll be fine." Matt looked at her, his eyes narrowing slightly. "Unless there's a reason you don't want him here."

"You'd probably like peace and quiet."

He looked at the little boy. "I think conversation would be best this morning."

Alexandre beamed. He pulled out the chair across from Matt and sat down. "I can eat here, Mama." He looked at Matt. "We're going to *La Fête de la Victoire de 1945* together. There'll be lots to see. Did you want to come with us?"

"No," Jeanne-Marie said. "We're meeting Michelle and Marc and Pierre, remember?"

"But Matt would like them. Marc is big like him.

Then we would all have a friend at the parade. Michelle and Marc, me and Pierre, and you and Matt. It'll be good, Mama."

"I'm sure Matt has already made plans for the day," she said. "I'll get your breakfast. Don't be pestering him."

"Did you make plans?" Alexandre asked when his mother walked away.

"I was going for a climb," Matt said. Truth be told, he had planned to do another climb not as challenging as he'd been doing. He was getting a later start than he wanted, due to a sleepless night.

But as he ate and listened to Alexandre's chatter, he thought more about changing plans and going with the Rousseaus to the fete. Would Jeanne-Marie be amenable? Or would she rather not mingle her guests and friends? She'd gone quickly to her quarters yesterday after they'd returned to the inn, saying she needed to soak in a hot bath.

He'd gone to town to eat and hadn't seen her again until this morning.

Alexandre bounced on his chair. "I love fetes. I like the food and the parades. And all the people. Sometimes I can't see everything because I'm little, but then Mama picks me up to see better. Pierre's dad picks him up really high. Mama can't pick me up so high. You are very tall. You could pick me up highest."

"If I were going with you."

"Can you, please?"

When Jeanne-Marie returned from the kitchen with Alexandre's breakfast, both of them at the table looked at her. "Mama, Matt is going with us to the fete and he'll lift me up high to see!"

Jeanne-Marie's eyes widened and she stared at him. "You're going with us?"

"If you don't wish me to lift him, I won't. But he would be higher, don't you think?"

She nodded, putting the plate in front of Alexandre, trying to understand what was going on. "I thought you were climbing."

"I can climb tomorrow."

Jeanne-Marie didn't know what to say. How would she spend the entire day in close proximity to Matthieu Sommer?

They left the inn just before ten o'clock. Alexandre was beside himself, racing out in front, then running back to urge them on. Jeanne-Marie was careful to keep a distance between herself and the stern-looking man walking beside her. He had not smiled again like he had yesterday. If anything, he seemed to regret it. Still, he was going with her today. She wondered what Michelle would think when she showed up with him.

The small coastal town was already crowded with colorful booths lining both sides of the main street, which had been closed for the day. Everything imaginable was for sale, from fresh warm cookies to scarves, sunglasses, wood carvings, brassware, and original paintings and crafts of every kind. When they began to be jostled by others, Jeanne-Marie took hold of Alexandre's hand so he wouldn't get separated from her in the growing crowd.

The tricolor flew on every lamppost and by each booth. The joy in the day was evident by the happy revelers. It was a perfect day.

Or would be if she could enjoy herself instead of being so very aware of the man walking at her side. She was getting too interested in her guest. Surrounded by the crowd, she still felt as if she and Matt were almost alone. She had to pay attention to what else was going on around her.

Matt studied the scene from time to time, looking wherever Alexandre pointed. They passed a juggler mesmerizing his audience. A small band played near the town center, with people crowding the sidewalks to enjoy the music.

They stopped at every booth. Matt wondered if the entire day was going to be silent, with Jeanne-Marie not speaking. He reached out and took her arm, stopping her.

She turned and stared at him with wide eyes.

"If you don't wish for me to accompany you, please say so."

"Of course you can come with us. You're here, aren't you?"

"And you haven't said one word since we left the inn. Which leads me to surmise you'd just as soon wish I was a million miles away."

She shook her head. "No, I'm glad you came with us. It's just—" She shrugged. "I don't know, I feel a bit funny if you want the truth. This is the first time I've attended anything with a man since Phillipe died. It feels awkward. I know this isn't a date or anything," she rushed in to explain. "But others might look on it as if it were and then I'd have to explain and there's nothing to explain, but it gets complicated."

He nodded. "I get it. This is the first time I've attended anything since my family died, too. It is different. It's not what either of us thought we'd be doing today, but let's give Alexandre a good day. Let others think what they want."

She nodded, relieved he understood. And for her, nothing was more important than letting her son enjoy himself.

Except—today she wanted Matt to enjoy himself as well. He'd lived with heartache too long.

"You and I know the truth, so what does it matter what others think?" he asked, leaning closer so she could hear him. Feeling the brush of his breath across her face, her eyes grew even wider as she stared right back at him. Matt was shocked at the sudden spurt of awareness and desire that shot through him.

His gaze dropped to her lips and she instinctively licked them. He felt another shot of desire deep inside. Time seemed to stand still. Alexandre had nothing to do with the sensations he was feeling now.

Clearing her throat, Jeanne-Marie dragged her gaze away and turned to look at the booth they stood in front of. "This is a fine example of local wood carving," she said, her voice husky.

It took a moment for him to be able to move. He was stunned he could feel anything after Marabelle's death. He took a step back and gave his attention to the vendor, who tried to convince them they needed an assortment of wooden animals. Blood pounded in his veins. He glanced around, but no one else in the crowd noticed anything unusual. No one picked up on his reaction. No one could condemn him for normal male reactions to a pretty woman.

"We don't buy, we just look," Alexandre said. "Too much stuff to carry," he said gravely.

Glad for the boy's comment, Matt drew in a deep breath, avoiding looking at Jeanne-Marie. "Maybe on the way home we can find a memento of the day," Matt told the boy. Keep things impersonal. And keep

Alexandre between them. He'd focus on the little boy and make sure he had a good time.

They met Jeanne-Marie's friends at the designated corner shortly before the parade was to begin. Michelle couldn't hide her surprise when she saw Matt accompanying Jeanne-Marie and Alexandre, but she tried to cover it up, rushing to introduce her son and husband. Alexandre and Pierre were friends and began talking about what they hoped was going to be in the parade.

When more and more people pressed in around them, Matt knew the parade was about to begin. He lifted Alexandre into his arms so he could see more than waists and legs. As a defense mechanism it wasn't foolproof, but it kept his attention focused on the parade and the boy and not the woman standing beside him. When others moved to crowd into the remaining space, Jeanne-Marie had to step closer. He could smell her perfume, light and airy, and as much a part of her as her dark hair. She was no longer so distant, and he wasn't sure if that was good or bad. At least when she wasn't talking to him, he had been okay. Now he grew more aware of her every second.

"I'm up high," Alexandre said gleefully, leaning over to see Pierre, whose father had also lifted him.

"Me, too," Pierre said with laughter.

The first entry in the parade was an eclectic band, the national anthem played at the midway point of the parade route. Then the musicians played marching music as they continued down the street.

Following were homemade floats, decorated cars with people waving, a dancing group from a local school. A high school band, and assorted veteran companies dressed in uniform, cheered by the spectators. A fire truck followed, blowing its siren from time to time and spraying the crowd with a fine mist of water.

When the parade ended forty-five minutes later, Michelle and Marc invited Jeanne-Marie and Matt to join them for lunch.

"No. I need to get back to the inn," Jeanne-Marie said.

"Why?" Michelle asked. "You have Rene to keep an eye on things, and all your guests are surely here."

Jeanne-Marie turned slightly so Matt couldn't see her face and rolled her eyes in his direction.

Michelle grinned and leaned closer. "To be alone with him?"

"No!" Jeanne-Marie said, horrified. This was just the kind of conclusion she was afraid her friend would jump to. "I can't tie him up all day," she said softly.

"I want to ride the merry-go-round," Alexandre said.

"We usually do let the children ride," Michelle said, her eyes dancing at Jeanne-Marie's discomfort.

"Is there a carousel?" Matt asked Jeanne-Marie. She turned and nodded, giving up on her plan to flee back to the inn and barricade herself into her private rooms.

"There's a traveling carnival at the edge of town, in one of the lots set back from the sea. It'll be jammed with kids, though."

"I'm a firm believer in letting children enjoy life as much as they can while they can." And it would delay return to the inn. He would spend the entire day surrounded by the crowd if he could. He did not want to be alone with either Jeanne-Marie—or his thoughts.

"Okay, thank you, he'll love it."

Time passed swiftly. Despite his best efforts to remain distant, Matt caught himself darting glances her way. Her laugher was contagious. Her delight in mundane things had him looking at the world in a new light. Everything seemed lighter than before, more colorful. Even the heightened sense of awareness that did not diminish as the day went on. He wondered if she picked up on it. She was careful to keep out of touching distance. Though once or twice the crowded walkway jostled her so she bumped into him. He let his fingers linger just a second when steadying her. Her skin was soft as silk.

Jeanne-Marie knew most of the people in town and was frequently greeted. She in turn introduced Matt, mentioning only that he was visiting to climb Les Calanques. She ignored the occasional look of speculation.

By three o'clock Alexandre was definitely tired. He rested his head on Matt's shoulder and stopped talking.

"You all right, Alexandre?" he asked.

"I'm tired," he said.

"He usually naps most days. I'll take him back to the inn. It's been wonderful. I haven't had this much fun in a long time. Thank you, Matt, for seeing it with us. I hope you enjoyed it as well," she said, her eyes darting to his, then back to Alexandre.

"I'll go back with you. This little guy isn't going to be wanting to walk and he's too heavy for you to carry all that way." There was still time to get in a short climb. Preferably very steep and strenuous. Something to take his mind off the woman at his side.

"Thank you."

The three of them headed for the inn. To a casual observer they probably looked like a young family, husband, wife and child. For a split second Matt felt a pang that it wasn't so. Then reason returned. He was not looking to replace his family with another. He was not going to fall in love again. Life was too uncertain to risk everything by falling in love, having his life on edge awaiting another fateful outcome.

When they reached the veranda, Matt let Jeanne-Marie take Alexandre, who was almost asleep.

"Thank you," she said again.

"No problem."

He handed off the boy. When she went to their quarters, he took the stairs to his room.

Quickly changing into climbing clothes, he headed out.

She was talking to Rene when he descended. She looked up.

"Going for a climb? Isn't it a bit late?"

"I'll find a short climb, check out the view from another vantage point," he said, and kept walking. He would drive himself to the point of exhaustion so he'd sleep. And he'd get his head on straight. He might find some physical attraction to the pretty innkeeper, but he wasn't going there. She was a forever-after kind of woman, and he'd not risk his very soul again on ephemeral love.

Jeanne-Marie watched as he left, a spring in his step, his look anticipatory.

She brushed her fingertips across her lips, remembering their kiss. She'd pushed the thought away during the day, but now the memory returned. She had felt a pull of attraction that was as strong as any she'd ever had for Phillipe. Once when he'd leaned over her to say something, she'd thought he was going to kiss her again.

But she'd misread the situation. Matt had turned away

and the moment had been lost. Not that she forgot it. Doing her best to keep her distance the rest of the day, she still felt an awareness that bordered on the edge of obsession. He was the perfect tall, dark and handsome man romance novels so loved. His body was honed to perfection. His smile didn't reach his eyes, but still had the ability to stir her heart.

"Which is foolishness," she said aloud, to Rene's confusion.

"Pardon?"

"Rien." Shaking her head, she went to prepare a pitcher of lemonade and then to sit on the veranda. She'd enjoy the rest of the day no matter what! Alexandre would probably sleep till dinnertime, which was good, so he would keep awake for the fireworks. Softly she sighed as she looked across the beach to the sea. Spending the evening on the veranda and watching the pyrotechnics from the comfort of the inn was the perfect way to end the day. The fireworks were shot over the water, so the veranda offered a perfect vantage point. Since she had taken over running the inn, Jeanne-Marie had invited all her guests as well.

It was a nice tradition, she thought, and kept the memories of Phillipe alive.

It had taken a while, but now she knew she wouldn't fall apart if she remembered happy times with him. More often than not, now she was angry at his taking foolish risks and leaving her and Alexandre behind. She knew her loss and his couldn't be measured by how or why. Only the aching emptiness where love once flourished.

She felt restless, and sitting still had all sorts of thoughts crowding her mind. Ones she didn't want. Again her thoughts went to Matthieu Sommer.

This had to stop.

She popped in to tell Rene she was going for a walk and would be back soon.

Stepping off onto the sand, Jeanne-Marie took off her sandals and looped them through her fingers, heading directly to the sea and the packed sand where the water kissed the shore.

Then, as if unable to stop herself, she turned to walk toward Les Calanques. It wasn't that she expected to run into Matt on his return, but if she did, then they could talk as they walked back to the inn.

She studied the crags and cliffs ahead of her. How Phillipe had loved them for the short climbs he could take on weekends. And she'd enjoyed spending time with his grandfather while they waited for him to return.

Yesterday had been amazing. She'd actually climbed a cliff. Granted, it wasn't very high or steep, but it was more than she'd ever done before. And Alexandre had loved it. He'd talked about it all last night. And had regaled Pierre today when they were watching the parade.

She knew Alexandre wanted to climb mountains one day. She hoped he'd outgrow the idea. But if not, could she stop him? She didn't want to coddle him. But the thought of him scaling a sheer face of rock had her almost in a panic. She wanted him to be proud of his father. Yet she didn't want him to necessarily follow entirely in Phillipe's footsteps.

By the time she reached the rocky area that led to the base of the cliffs, Jeanne-Marie knew she had to turn around. She needed to be home when Alexandre awoke. Just as she was about to turn, she saw Matt in the distance, gazing out to the sea. She stopped. Her inclination was to continue until she reached him. But he looked so intent, she didn't know if she should intrude.

She watched for a long time. Giving into temptation, she scrambled over the rocks and found the faint path at the base of the cliffs. Following it, she would reach him in no time. Then what would she say?

He saw her and turned to walk toward her.

"Out for a walk?" he asked when he was close enough to be heard.

"Alexandre's sleeping, so I thought I'd have a bit of time to myself."

"Ah, then I'll leave you to your walk."

"No. That's okay. I'm ready to head back. You looked like you were lost in thought gazing out at the sea."

"I was thinking about sailing around the world."

"Oh, wow, that's ambitious. I didn't know you sailed."

"A totally unrealistic thought since I've never sailed by myself. I think I'd like a competent crew and big boat that could handle anything the sea throws at us. Then maybe."

"Have you done any long distance sailing?"

"Around the Med a few summers ago as part of a crew. But my father was living then and in charge of the winery. Now, it falls primarily to me. The appeal of being on the water would be the total lack of communication. And that's unreal—decisions have to be made, plans implemented."

"So work up to a sabbatical like professors have," she said, falling into step with him.

"Hmm. In the meantime, climbing's a strong leader for most desired escape."

She laughed. "What happened to quiet, safe hobbies

like stamp collecting or photography?" She felt almost giddy around him.

He tilted his head slightly. "I might consider taking a picture from the top of a climb."

"If the camera didn't get banged up on the way."

"Never happen."

"Have you ever fallen?" she asked.

"Slipped a few times. No harm done."

"That's a blessing."

"Not all climbers fall," he said.

"I know that. But there have to be less scary hobbies."

"Sure, but what could compare?"

"Travel, for one."

"Where would you like to travel?" he asked.

"London," she answered promptly.

"And what's there?"

"Everything. From Westminster Abbey to the London Eye."

"Would you be brave enough to ride in it?" he asked.

"Hey, I'm adventuresome. I came to France from America, didn't I? I climbed a cliff yesterday. I imagine the view from the top of the Eye would be spectacular."

"Probably. The view from the top of the cliffs is spectacular. I'd hardly call what you scaled yesterday a cliff."

The teasing tone in his voice startled her. She looked at him suspiciously.

"Are you making fun of me?"

"No." But his lips twitched.

She remembered the grin he'd given her yesterday when she'd complained about the strain on her arms and legs. It would be worth being mocked to see him laugh.

The walk back took far less time than she expected. Alexandre was playing on the veranda and jumped up to run to her when he saw her.

"I'd like to take you and your son to dinner," Matt said just before the child reached them.

"What? You don't have to take us to dinner," she said quickly. Her interest couldn't be that blatant, could it?

"If you knew me better, you'd know I rarely do things I don't wish to. It would be a…a good ending to the day," Matt said as if choosing his words carefully.

"Mama, where were you? Rene said you'd be back but you've been gone a long time," Alexandre said when he reached her.

"I went for a walk. I thought you'd still be asleep. Now I'm back. Matt asked to take us out to dinner. Won't that be fun?"

"Shall we leave in about a half hour? That'll give me time to clean up a bit."

Jeanne-Marie nodded. She wanted to clean up a bit herself.

Once in her room, she debated what to wear. She loved the way her blue dress fit and showed off her figure. But was it too much when she'd been wearing khakis all day? Maybe the pink top, which gave color to her cheeks. She stared at herself in the mirror for a long moment. Who was that staring back? A widow living without her husband. A mother who loved her son.

But, just maybe, a woman on the brink of something different. Would it be wonderful or end up leaving her mourning what could never be? Funny, she hadn't thought about making a life with any other man. She'd loved Phillipe. She was trying to make her life what she thought he would have wanted. But he was gone. Maybe it was time to look for other ways to spend the future. Alexandre wouldn't be with her forever. He would grow up, go off to college and marry. He could live on another continent as she did, so far from where she grew up.

What would the years after that hold?

Right now was not the time to grow philosophical.

She chose the pink top to go with the khaki slacks. She would wear nicer shoes. Every restaurant would be mobbed because of the holiday. Casual was the dress of the day.

The excitement shining in her eyes couldn't be ignored. Was she ready for this?

"Do you like growing grapes and making wine?" Jeanne-Marie asked once they were finally seated in Le Chat Noir. The wait had seemed interminable, with Alexandre complaining every two minutes he was hungry. Most of the people waiting, however, had been in high spirits. The festive air permeated the village. Matt hadn't minded the wait. For the first time in a long while he felt connected with others.

"Is that something you always wanted to do?" she added.

"Ever since I was a kid, I knew this was my role in life. I enjoy it. And when I can take a vacation, it seems the best part is returning home. I can't imagine anything else I'd rather do. I suspect you never yearned to be an innkeeper." He thought of the acres of vineyards, the constant worry about the weather or pests. The heavy, laden vines just before harvest, the purple grapes looking almost frosted. He missed being there.

She laughed. Matt was struck again by the sound of her laughter. He let his gaze settle on her for a moment.

She looked lovely tonight with color in her cheeks and a sparkle in her eyes. He would like to hear that laughter more. He suspected that she didn't laugh nearly enough.

"Not at all. Before I met Phillipe, I planned to be an art historian, maybe teach. I enjoyed my classes at university and wanted to have others find the same delight in studying paintings by the masters. But once I fell in love, all I wanted was a family and a happy life. Strange how things worked out. Phillipe hadn't wanted to run the inn, but refused to sell it when his grandfather died. Even his mother suggested selling and it had been her childhood home. I never expected to own it myself and run it. Still, look how fortunate I am."

"Indeed." Making the best of the situation. Which he struggled to do as well.

After their order had been taken, he leaned back as Alexandre chattered away, talking about his day, the rides he'd gone on and the fact he'd seen all the parade since Matt had held him so high.

"Definitely a wonderful thing," Jeanne-Marie said, wishing Phillipe had had more time with his son. Alexandre had been a baby when he died. He'd never known the joy of his conversation, his enchantment with life. And Alexandre would never know his father except by what Jeanne-Marie and his grandparents told him.

Matt leaned forward slightly. "No time for sadness. This is a celebration."

She looked up. "I'm sorry, I was thinking about his father and how much he missed. I really appreciate your coming today. Look how much he liked it."

Matt looked at Alexandre. "My son was that age when he was killed. Think of all he missed."

"Oh, you're right, this is not a time to grow melancholy.

Thank you for inviting us to dinner. Afterward, we'll head back, grab a good seat on the veranda and watch the fireworks. They are the highlight of the day for me. You'll love them."

Matt pushed away thoughts of another woman, another fete, and focused on the woman with him tonight. One evening didn't mean he'd forgotten his family any more than Jeanne-Marie had forgotten hers. They were both alive. Life was meant for the living.

Several of the guests at the inn were seated on the veranda by the time Jeanne-Marie, Matt and Alexandre returned. A few chairs were empty, which she asked him to stake out for them while she went to get the cookies and cakes she'd prepared earlier in the week for just this occasion. Soon everyone on the veranda was sipping iced lemonade and munching on the desserts.

The bursting of colorful fireworks was the perfect ending to the celebration. Jeanne-Marie couldn't remember a happier day since Phillipe died. She was growing more comfortable around Matt and appreciated his attention to her son. He must have been a great father to his own child. Would Phillipe have been as attentive and involved? He'd worked long hours, and gone climbing every chance he got. He hadn't curtailed his activities after Alexandre had been born, but as an infant, he wouldn't have been much company to his father. As he'd grown older, would Phillipe have included him?

No sense worrying about what might have been. Phillipe was gone. Never to return. And Matt? He was here today. Beyond that, she didn't care to look.

CHAPTER SIX

JEANNE-MARIE put Alexandre to bed, but she felt too restless and keyed up to sit quietly after the fireworks. She went back to the common area, straightening cushions and pillows here and there. Rene had taken off and she'd close up in another hour or so. Several of the guests had gone back to the village to enjoy dancing at one or two of the places that offered a band.

Wandering out onto the veranda a few minutes later, she was surprised to see Matt still sitting there. Feeling her heart lurch a bit, she went to join him.

"Not going back to town?" she asked as she sat beside him.

"Nothing there for me. Does the town always have such an amazing display of pyrotechnics?"

"A lot of the annual budget goes to them. Fabulous, I think."

There was a muffled boom in the distance and a faint glow in the sky.

"Marseilles is finishing up," she commented. "I remember a few years ago we were amazed with their display. But this suits me fine. I like not being in the midst of a huge crowd," she said, gazing out across the dark sea. In the distance a ship's lights could be seen, gliding toward the east.

"Do you go to Marseilles often?" he asked.

"Not as often as I probably ought to. Alexandre's grandparents live there and he visits them from time to time. I'm taking him over on Monday for a couple of days. I'll do some shopping while I'm there, but pretty much St. Bart suits all our needs."

"What time are you taking him?"

"In the afternoon. Why?"

"I could drive you both and then take you to dinner."

Jeanne-Marie tried to see his expression in the faint light spilling from the French doors. But his face was in shadow. Another dinner? She swallowed hard. They would drop Alexandre off at his grandparents. It would just be the two of them. No matter how she thought about tonight, a dinner in Marseilles, just the two of them, would be a date.

A touch of panic. Was she ready for such a step? Not that it meant more than two people enjoying a meal together. He hadn't asked her to run away with him.

"Why?" she blurted out.

"As a thank-you for your hospitality."

"I'm an innkeeper, you're a guest. Nothing beyond payment for your room is needed." She felt deflated. It was merely a thank-you. She'd thought he meant more.

"Then, because I'd enjoy sharing another meal with you. I'd like to spend a bit more time together before I head for home."

Her heart sped up a little. "Just you and me?"

"Unless you wish to take Alexandre to his grandparents later. Then he could eat with us," Matt said easily.

It would be less like a date if Alexandre were with

them. But—there was nothing wrong with having a meal with a guest. Especially on his last day. She would view it as the thank-you gesture he said initially.

"He should go to his grandparents first. And yes, I'd like to have dinner with you." The minute she said it, she wished she could snatch back the words. It was a date! She hadn't dated in years. She never thought she would again, at least not until she was over Phillipe's death. Which she wasn't. Yet. Or was she?

"Maybe I'll extend my stay another few days," he said.

She tried to remember future reservations. "I think I'm booked," she said finally, feeling disappointed. This seesaw of emotions confused her. Did she want to see where a relationship between them could lead or not?

She did. She'd have to double-check reservations. If there was a way to keep a room for Matt, she would find it.

"Ah, I hadn't thought about that. Maybe I'll have to look for something elsewhere in the village."

"I can double-check." She made a move to stand, but his hand caught hers and tugged her back down. The tingling that shot through her arm was pleasant, tanta-lizing. She looked at him, feeling his hand imprinted as if she'd never forget.

"Time enough in the morning. Let's just enjoy the evening. If the rooms are all booked, so be it. I'll take you to dinner and then head for home."

"That would be so late."

"Or we could get rooms in Marseilles and I'll drive you back in the morning and then head for home."

That raised all sorts of concerns. Jeanne-Marie took a deep breath and shook her head, much as she was tempted. Not that he was suggesting a single room. She caught her breath at the thought. His kiss had knocked her off her senses; what would making love be like?

She grew warm thinking about it, glad for the darkness to hide her face. She was probably beet-red by now.

"No, I have to prepare breakfast for my guests. I have to return home Monday night, no matter how late."

"Of course."

It was a beautiful evening with a soft breeze blowing from the sea and she was sitting with a gorgeous man. His hand had slid down her arm and now held her hand loosely in his. The focal point of her existence was on their linked hands. She couldn't think about anything else except Matt and the wild feelings that exploded in her when he touched her. A million women would trade places with her in a heartbeat. How had she been so lucky?

In a desperate attempt to stop thinking about unlikely possibilities, she asked, "What was your favorite part of today?" Her entire body seemed attuned to Matt. She could stay here forever. The darkness sheltered them. The gaiety in the town was a sweet background melody that mingled with the soft sighing of the sea as it brushed the sand. For a time, cares seemed forgotten. The past faded away, the future was unknown. She had only this moment.

"The food. I bet we sampled two dozen different dishes. How that boy of yours kept eating is amazing to me."

"He has his moments. I hope it all goes to making him a tall man. My father isn't very tall. I want Alexandre to be tall like his father."

"Tell me about Phillipe," Matt invited.

She hesitated. She disliked the way people tiptoed

around the subject, but now that it was broached, what could she say? She didn't want to talk about him to Matt. Yet, he was such an important part of her life. "He was tall, with brown hair, looked a bit like his father, whom you met. He had the most amazing vitality. He was always on the go. I used to wonder how he had the patience to scale the sheer cliffs he did. It takes careful study and patience to pick out the best route. He always seemed antsy, always looking for things to do. He didn't sit still very often." She didn't bother to reveal he had also been a bit of a show-off, talking about exploits he'd done, bragging about future climbs he planned. The more daring, the more he liked talking about them.

"Did you two have a house?"

"No, a large flat near the water in Marseilles. He made a good living and supported us well. The place seemed so empty after he died. I sold it when we moved here."

"What was your favorite holiday?"

Jeanne-Marie thought about it for a moment. Did none stand out? "We usually went wherever he was going to climb. I don't climb, as you saw the other day, so I found things to do in the towns or villages where we stayed. I liked Italy. He climbed in the Italian Alps one time and I enjoyed the village he used as base. He never wanted to spend the time sightseeing when he could be climbing."

"And that suited you?"

"Well, a real dream holiday would be pampering, breakfast in bed, then a day of shopping, maybe a play in the evening or a fabulous dinner somewhere with dancing," she said dreamily. "But for the time being, I think Alexandre and I will be content to stay here. You have to admit, it's beautiful right on the sea. I do love living by the water."

"You should come visit the Loire Valley sometime. Especially in spring. It's beautiful, as well."

Matt hoped when she checked the reservations tomorrow that he'd be able to stay. Paul would be returning home soon. Not that it mattered much to him. The one climb they'd done together hadn't been as relaxing or challenging as the others this week. Paul's idea of recreation was more clubbing and less climbing.

He thought about Jeanne-Marie's husband. Granted, he understood the appeal of taking vacations to climb. But surely at one point in their marriage he would have wanted to go where she wanted. Not that Matt was going to pass an opinion on their marriage. Jeanne-Marie had loved the man and grieved his death.

Not liking the trend of his thoughts, he glanced at her. She seemed so serene. He liked that the most about her, he thought. Not that her laughter wasn't infectious. Or the special way she looked at a person when he talked, like he was the only other person in the world. Her hand was smaller than his, felt delicate and warm in his. Contentment seeped in. It was comfortable sitting on the veranda in the dark.

Then the thought of kissing her rose and wouldn't be pushed away. Would she be willing? One way to find out.

He gave her hand a gentle squeeze and released it. "I'm heading for bed. I'm making another climb tomorrow. You can let me know when I get back if I can stay another few days."

She jumped up, almost pressing against him she was

so close. "I'd better get some sleep myself. Dawn comes early and breakfast doesn't make itself."

"Before we go in..." he said, drawing her into his arms, slowly so as to give her time to back out if she wanted. She didn't.

When his mouth found hers, her kiss was sweet. Her lips were warm, opening to his without hesitation. Deepening his kiss he felt her response, passion with passion, pressing against him with her body as if wanting to get as close to him as he wanted to get to her. Desire spiraled, senses went into overload. Her curves inflamed him. Her softness made him that much harder. Matt could only feel the hunger increase. He wanted her. She was all he wanted right now. The rest of the world faded until only the two of them existed in the darkness. Would she come to his room with him?

The thought shocked him. He pulled back, trying to see her in the faint light. She gazed up at him, her expression impossible to read. Kissing her on her cheek, trailing down to her neck and back up the other side to that cheek, he breathed in the scent of her, tasted that soft skin, heard her ragged breathing as she held him tightly in her embrace.

Reluctantly he rested his forehead against hers. He didn't know what he wanted. Making love with her would take him in a direction he never thought to go. Was it too soon for him? For her?

He'd vowed never to be a hostage to fate again. The solo path was safer. If he could only clamp down on the roiling desire that rose.

"I need to go in," she said softly, her fingers brushing against his cheek. "I had a wonderful time today." When she pulled away, he let her go. And watched her walk into the inn.

He stared after her long moments after she left. His own breathing slowed.

He'd kissed her again, over and over, actually. And she'd responded.

Had she ever!

With a groan, he relived every second. She'd felt so feminine and utterly desirable. He'd thought that aspect of life was over, but her kisses proved him totally wrong.

Matt was down the next morning before the sun rose. The kitchen was still dark.

He continued on to his car, not wishing to meet up with Jeanne-Marie this morning. He needed some time to get his head on straight. He stopped by the bakery on his way to the base of the cliffs. Once the car was parked, he quickly walked along the path until he came to the one he planned to try. He paused at the base and scanned the face. No other climbers out yet, which could make the climb more dangerous in case of trouble.

Yet wasn't that why he pushed himself? Taking harder and harder climbs as if determined to triumph in one area of life. If fate had a different ending in mind, it would only end the sorrow that much sooner.

Dipping into his resin bag, he coated his fingers. He didn't feel as driven today as the previous days. A challenging climb, not a dangerous one, was what he was seeking today. The pamphlets he'd obtained from the inn and the sports shop in the village rated the climbs. This one promised to be only moderately difficult.

Reaching for the first handhold, he thought about Jeanne-Marie. Would last night's kisses have changed things between them? Did he want them to?

Pausing for a moment between reaching for handholds,

he leaned his forehead against the cool stone. He was not getting entangled with anyone ever again. He'd made that vow when he'd buried Marabelle and Etienne. So what was he doing kissing Jeanne-Marie?

The sun hadn't yet risen high enough to show every nook and cranny of the cliff face, but there was more than enough light to choose the best way up the seemingly flat face. He wanted a short climb, to get back to the inn. See her again.

Climbing took concentration, an awareness of where he was and what his next move would be. Forcing other thoughts away helped him remain focused. Yet from time to time his attention lapsed and he wished he'd found out before he'd left this morning if the room was available next week. If she would have been glad to see him, or was feeling awkward.

This was as bad as being a teenager with overzealous hormones. He kept thinking about Jeanne-Marie. Last night had not been enough. He wanted more.

Reaching the summit sometime later, he lay back on the warmed rock and closed his eyes, immediately seeing her face. Maybe staying longer wasn't the wisest move he could make. But for the first time in a long while he felt alive. He didn't want to cut it short. The aching pain of loss had diminished. He would never forget, but he could move on. Just like people had said.

He remembered some of the comments Alexandre had made at the fair and laughed out loud. Then he remembered kissing Jeanne-Marie and almost groaned. Just thinking about her had him longing to get back to the inn to see her. He sat up and began eating lunch, gazing across the sparkling blue of the Mediterranean.

Despite his best intentions to segregate himself from the world, Matt was being brought out of the past and into the present. Each time they were together, Alexandre said something funny. And the hero worship he had was special. Matt dared not do anything to tarnish that. It was healing to find he could be a role model to an impressionable child.

It was Jeanne-Marie who had him thinking of kisses and caresses and wanting to spend time together, at dinner, sitting on the veranda. Wherever she was.

Jeanne-Marie sat at the desk, totaling all the figures for the past week. Three couples had checked out. Two more were due to arrive before dark. And the couple in the suite had left a huge tip, which she put right into Alexandre's college fund. When he grew up there'd be money for university, or whatever else he might wish to do. In the meantime, they were comfortable.

The numbers blurred and once again she was on the veranda reliving the kisses she and Matt had shared last night. Looking up and out to the sea, she again felt the sensations that had swamped her. Desire, heat, longing. She loved his kisses. She loved the feelings she had when he held her. Feeling as if she'd wakened from a long sleep, she relished every tiny aspect. She had thought about those kisses far into the night, unable to sleep as she fretted about her reaction. She'd been late with breakfast, barely having the first batch of warm bread out of the oven when guests came to the dining room.

Now she was alone and again the memory of his warm lips demanding a response from her captured her thoughts and wouldn't turn loose. She was still surprised at the delight that had splashed through her. Unable to wrap her mind around her own response, she brushed her fingertips across her lips. Was she ready to look beyond her life with Phillipe and into a different future than she'd once thought she'd have?

She heard a car in the parking lot and involuntarily her heart rate increased. Was it Matt? Wiping her hands on her khaki slacks, she watched the corner of the veranda, anticipating the moment she'd see him again. She'd missed him that morning. Almost laughing at herself, she remembered going straight to the reservation book before even starting breakfast.

He came around the corner onto the veranda and strode toward one of the open French doors. Stepping inside, he spotted her instantly. Jeanne-Marie caught her breath, forced herself to exhale and then smiled. The memory of their kisses sprang to the forefront. It was all she could do to bravely meet his eyes. He didn't have second thoughts, did he? She didn't know what to think when she realized he'd left this morning before she could see him.

"Good climb?" She was pleased her voice sounded normal. She hoped he didn't see signs of her rapidly beating heart.

"Excellent. Did you check reservations?" The intense way he looked at her convinced her he was also thinking of those kisses. No second thoughts. His dark eyes searched hers, his gaze touching on her lips.

She licked them nervously. "Yes. I was booked, but amazingly, around ten this morning, one of the reservations was canceled. You can stay another few days if you still want to."

He walked to the counter and leaned over it slightly. Jeanne-Marie saw the tanned face, the dark eyes focused on her with faint lines radiating from the edges. She could smell sunshine on him. Was he going to kiss her again?

"I do want. And we're on for tomorrow night?" His voice was low and vibrant. His gaze held hers and it was all she could do to respond to the question. Her fingers ached to reach out and trace those firm lips, test the strength of that strong jaw, feel the warmth of his suntanned skin.

She nodded. She had to clear her throat before she could speak. "I thought we'd leave around three, drop Alexandre off and then have an early dinner?"

"Works for me. Where is he?" He surveyed the room, then glanced out to the beach.

"He's at Pierre's house for the afternoon. Michelle and I trade back and forth having the kids. Today they're building a ramp for their cars to race. Marc's into wood-working and said he'd help the boys. I suspect it'll be more he'll do it and they'll be the ones clamoring to help."

"He likes those cars. Think he'll be a race driver?"

"I want him to be an accountant or something," she murmured. She couldn't look away. His eyes still held hers. She wished she didn't have the counter between them.

He laughed and her breath caught again. His laughter was rich and masculine and made him look younger, definitely happier. It was the first time she'd seen him laugh. Her heart ached to think how little he'd had to laugh about in the last two years. She smiled in delight, hoping he would find more to bring happiness in the future.

"He'll be what he'll be," Matt said. He reached out and touched her nose. "You can't keep him from doing what he wants, even if it's racing. If that makes him happy and being an accountant doesn't, which would you choose?"

"I want him to be happy. But preferably happy for a long, long time." She liked Matt's familiar touch. It made last night seem less like an aberration and maybe the beginning of something.

Two of the new guests arrived on the veranda. Jeanne-Marie could have screamed in frustration. Matt glanced over his shoulder, then told her he'd see her later and took the stairs two at a time. Jeanne-Marie turned to watch him before she greeted her guests. She wished she could shift into full innkeeper mode. But part of her couldn't let go of Matt.

She walked over to Michelle's house to get Alexandre before dinner. Visiting briefly with her friends, she and her son then walked home, with him talking a mile a minute about the ramp Pierre's father had built for their cars.

"And mine won almost every time. Pierre's going to get a new one so he can beat me, but today I won," her son explained on the way home.

"That's good. Next time maybe Pierre will win."

"Is Matt at home?" Alexandre asked when they reached the inn. "I want to tell him about the ramp."

"Yes, he's back from climbing." She wondered what he'd been doing since he returned. He had not come back downstairs after she'd checked in the new arrivals. "He's in his room, but you wait until he comes downstairs before talking to him. Do not disturb him in his room," she said.

"I won't 'sturb him, but he'll want to know about my ramp," Alexandre said earnestly.

"Nonetheless, you wait for him to come down."

Alexandre pouted and walked over to flop on one of the sofas in the lounge area.

CHAPTER SEVEN

JEANNE-MARIE prepared a thick soup and crusty bread for their dinner. By the time dinner was ready, Alexandre was in a better mood, but still impatient to see Matt. For that matter, so was she. She hoped it didn't show as much as it did with Alexandre.

"Tomorrow you're going to your grandparents' house for the night," she said as she set the small table in the alcove for their dinner.

"Can I take my cars?"

"Of course. Your grandfather will want to see them race side by side."

"Maybe we can go climbing. Do you think Matt would take me again?"

"Maybe." She wouldn't mind trying it herself again, as long as it was with Matt. Who would ever think she'd find anything redeeming in climbing rocks?

"Matt!" Alexandre scooped up his cars and ran to the kitchen doorway. "We built a ramp and our cars went really fast." He hugged the man's leg and looked up at him, his eyes shining.

Jeanne-Marie looked as well, wondering if she had that same look of adoration her son wore.

"Fantastic, I want to hear all about it," Matt said,

stooping to be on eye level with Alexandre. "Did yours win?"

"Yes. But Mama said next time maybe Pierre's will win. But mine's really fast."

"Life is not always about winning, but it's great when we do," Matt replied, his gaze moving to Jeanne-Marie.

"We're having soup and bread for dinner," she said. "There's plenty if you want to eat with us." She held her breath, hoping he'd say yes.

The faint flush of color on her cheeks could have been from the stove's heat, or it could mean something else. Matt nodded and rose, walking with Alexandre to the small square table, three chairs on three sides and the fourth side pressed to the wall beneath the window that overlooked the garden.

In only moments, Jeanne-Marie had served them all and sat down opposite Matt, Alexandre in the center.

The boy talked as fast as he could until his mother said, "Enough. Eat before the soup gets cold. Then you can finish telling Matt about your racing adventures."

Alexandre scowled but picked up his spoon. "But Matt needs to hear."

"When you're done eating," Matt said. He looked at Jeanne-Marie. "Are you full again? I heard people climbing up and down the stairs."

"More than full. One couple has a baby they didn't tell me about. I hope it doesn't cry in the night."

"Do you not let rooms to babies?" Matt asked.

Jeanne-Marie nodded, watching to see if he liked the meal. The soup had been simmering all afternoon, so thick with vegetables and beef it was almost a stew. The fresh, crusty bread had been made that morning. It was a simple meal, but one she took pride in. He seemed to like it.

"If I know in advance, I usually give families with small children the end room above the kitchen. There's a small storage room separating it from other rooms in the back, so crying babies aren't so noticeable. But they have the room smack in the center of the front, flanked by two other rooms." She shrugged. "I'll have a better idea if it's going to work by tomorrow. Here's hoping the baby sleeps through the night."

"I'm all done," Alexandre said, tipping his bowl slightly so his mother could see it was empty. "Now can I talk?"

Matt smiled at his impatience. Just like Etienne had been. He flicked a glance at Jeanne-Marie, raising an eyebrow in silent question.

She nodded solemnly. "Now you may talk."

"I have to go to my grandparents' tomorrow," he said, almost bouncing in his chair. "Will you still be here when I get back? We could walk along the beach again. Or I could go climbing with you," he ended hopefully.

"Yes, Matt will be here when you get back," Jeanne-Marie said.

"You'll have fun at your grandparents', right?" Matt asked.

"Sure, we'll go have ice cream and play in the park and watch movies on television. They have a television. We don't. Do you have a television?"

"I do."

Alexandre's eyes widened. "That's cool. I wish we had a television."

"Think what a treat it is when you go to your grandparents'," his mother said.

"She says I look like my dad," he told Matt.

He looked up at Jeanne-Marie, a question in his eyes.

"He looks a lot like Phillipe did at that age from the pictures I've seen. I'm sure Adrienne is constantly reminded." She looked at her son and Matt knew she was constantly reminded of her husband as well when she looked at him.

Which was worse, to have purged his house of reminders or to be constantly reminded by just looking at her son?

"Maybe they can take me to ride horses so I can learn. Then I can come visit you, Matt, and ride your horses."

"Maybe."

Jeanne-Marie threw him a look that was difficult to interpret.

"What?"

"We're not coming to visit, so don't raise his hopes."

"You'd be welcome," he said. Thinking about it for a moment, he realized he'd like to have her and her son come to see where he lived, where he worked. What would they think of his family's enterprise?

"Do you want some more soup?" she asked, clearly changing the subject.

"Yes. And more of that delicious bread."

After dinner Matt suggested a walk along the beach. While he saw no benefit from lying in the broiling sun all day, he did like being by the sea. The air was fresh and invigorating. She wouldn't go without her son, which suited him. Matt was surprised to realize he enjoyed Alexandre's company.

"A short walk, perhaps. We have to get ready for Alexandre's trip," she said, hesitating.

"Instead of going later, shall we leave in the morning

and have lunch together in Marseilles before dropping Alexandre off at his grandparents'?" Matt asked.

Alexandre looked at him. "Are you going to Marseilles, too?"

"I'm driving you to your grandparents' place," Matt said.

"Yea!" Alexandre danced around. "And will you pick me up, too?"

"If it's okay with your mother." And with that, Jeanne-Marie knew nothing could be better.

"We need to return soon so Alexandre can take a bath before bed," she said an hour later when they reached the marina. Twilight was near. It would take a while to walk back along the curving beach to get to the inn.

"If I swim in the sea I wouldn't need to take a bath," the little boy said, running ahead, then running back to be with them.

"Would you read me a story tonight?" he asked Matt, slipping his hand into the man's larger one.

It was startling. The child was without pretension. He said whatever came into his mind. Holding his hand, Matt was swept away with a feeling of protectiveness toward the little boy. How unfair life had been, losing his father when so young. Who would teach him how to be a man?

The sun had set only moments before. Twilight afforded plenty of light to see. The soft murmur of wavelets against the sand was soothing. Stars had not yet appeared but undoubtedly would before they reached the inn.

With Alexandre between them, each holding one of his hands, Matt thought how like a family they must appear. The thought came more and more frequently. He railed against it. He was on holiday. That was all.

Looking over at Jeanne-Marie, he was struck by her air of serenity. Content with her life, happy with her child, she cast a spell over him. He wanted that serenity, that contentment.

"Can we go swimming after dark?" Alexandre asked as they approached the inn.

"Not safe," his mother replied.

"Not dangerous, either. It could be fun," Matt said. He'd love to go swimming with Jeanne-Marie, to see her sleek body in a swimsuit, to touch her, to kiss her again. To feel her body against his, skin to skin.

He took a breath and shook his head trying to dislodge the images.

She looked dubious. "Maybe."

"Can we?" Alexandre was thrilled at the thought.

Matt looked at Jeanne-Marie. "Why not?" He could think of a dozen reasons to go, all starting with his motivation for the swim.

"Okay, let's do it."

"Yippee!" Alexandre yelled and took off running for the inn.

In less than ten minutes they had changed and were at the water's edge. Suddenly shy, Jeanne-Marie hesitated to take off her cover-up. The swimsuit she wore was the one she wore all the time. It maintained her modesty, but she felt exposed wearing it in front of him. She knew she was self-conscious because of Matt. Good heavens, it was almost pitch-dark out.

"Hurry, Mama," Alexandre called, already up to his knees in the water.

"Last one in's a rotten egg," Matt murmured, dropping his towel and walking toward Alexandre.

In one movement, she drew off her top, dropped it and ran by Matt, splashing into the water seconds before he did.

She kept going until the water was up to her waist.

"Wait for me, Mama."

Alexandre swam out to her and grabbed hold of her shoulders. "This is fun."

There was enough light now from the stars and the establishments along the shore to give some visibility. It was an adventure, however, to find the water so dark. Normally it was as clear as crystal with the bottom clearly visible.

Matt walked over. "Refreshing."

"Cold, you mean," she said. It was cool, but pleasant. And the delight of her son made it well worth it.

"Since he can swim, why don't we paddle a little out and then back?"

"Okay."

"I want to swim next to Matt," Alexandre said.

Me, too, was Jeanne-Marie's immediate thought.

They swam a short way, and because of the gentle slope Matt could stand when they stopped. Alexandre clung to him while Jeanne-Marie trod water beside him.

"If you get tired, you can grab hold of me," he offered.

She was tempted.

"It's scary out here," Alexandre said, looking around.

"No different from being here in the daytime except we can't see," Matt said.

Jeanne-Marie brushed against Matt's arm as she was moving around. He caught her and pulled her close. Resting her hand on his shoulder, she felt the warmth of his skin even though the water had cooled the surface.

Clinging, she smiled at her son.

"We've never done this before, have we?" She dared not look at Matt for fear she'd forget Alexandre was here and be caught up in Matt's spell. Would he kiss her again?

"I want to go back," Alexandre said.

When Matt put his arm around Jeanne-Marie's waist, she gasped. He drew her against his sleek body, the cooling effect of the water evaporating. She stared at him, wishing she could see him better. Her heart pounded as every inch of her became attuned to him. Heat matched heat and had her aware of him like never before. Her hands skimmed against his bare chest, feeling the muscles, his skin heating when she rested her palm against him.

For a moment she wished Alexandre was home in bed and just she and Matt were swimming in the darkened sea. Touching, kissing.

"We should go back," she said in a low voice. If it had been the two of them, she knew nothing would have stopped kisses and caresses.

So slowly she knew it was an effort, he released her, trailing his fingertips across her bare back, sending shivers up her spine.

"Race you, Alexandre," she said to cover her confusion. In a moment she was splashed by the little boy's wild swimming technique. This was her reality.

When they reached the shore, Matt right beside them, Alexandre ran onto the sand. "I beat!" He danced around and laughed. "That was fun!"

As Jeanne-Marie slowly climbed out of the water, heading for her towel, she could feel Matt's gaze on her and wished she dared turn around to feast her eyes on him. A spotlight on the beach would have been perfect. But first things first. She had her son to think about.

"No warm sun to dry us off," Matt commented, standing near her, watching her as she toweled off her body. She glanced his way, captivated by what she could see of his broad chest and muscular arms. He needed a lot of upper body strength to lift his body by his hands on climbs. She wished she had the courage to reach out and feel that strength. She looked away, yearnings firmly squashed.

"Can we do that again?" Alexandre asked.

"Not tonight. Time you got to bed. Tomorrow will be a big day," she said, pulling on the short cover-up. She wrung water from her hair and then looked at Matt again, vaguely disappointed he'd pulled on a T-shirt. So much for fantasies in the moonlight.

The next morning Alexandre bounced on the backseat of Matt's car. He seemed almost more excited to be in Matt's car than about his visit. Going to Marseilles with Matt felt like a big adventure to her, so she could empathize with her son's excitement. They'd deliver Alexandre to his grandparents after lunch and then she'd spend the rest of the afternoon and evening with Matt. Anticipation built. She wanted to rein it in, but no matter how much she tried, she couldn't squelch her excitement.

It was not a date. Not precisely. They'd have Alexandre with them for part of the day. It was the kindness of a guest to his hostess.

She didn't believe that for one second.

After lunch at a family-style restaurant, they arrived at the small home on the outskirts of town where the senior Rousseaus lived. Matt parked in front.

"Shall I carry his bag in?" he asked, turning slightly in the seat to look at the house.

"No. I'll just be a minute," Jeanne-Marie said. She could just imagine what spin Adrienne would put on seeing her with Matt. She didn't want to force her into acting like a gracious hostess. She'd deliver Alexandre and let his grandparents spoil him. While she went on her own adventure. "Tell Matt goodbye."

In seconds she took her son's hand and headed up the short walkway to the front door. She rang the bell. When she and Phillipe came to visit, he'd always walked right in, but she didn't feel comfortable doing that, though the Rousseaus had told her time and again she didn't need to stand on ceremony.

"Ah, Alexandre, you're here!" Adrienne threw open the door and greeted her grandson with a bright smile and big hug. "I thought you might be here earlier. I called the inn to get an exact time and your clerk said you'd already left."

"We ate lunch with Matt," Alexandre said, turning to wave at the car.

Adrienne looked beyond them to the car, her smile fading. "I see. I thought he was a guest at the inn." She looked at Jeanne-Marie with worry in her eyes.

"He is. He offered to drive us here today. He has a friend in Marseilles also vacationing," Jeanne-Marie said, feeling guilty.

"So you don't wish to come in," Adrienne said.

"I don't think I should keep him waiting," Jeanne-Marie said. This was more awkward than she'd anticipated. What if Adrienne thought she was dating again?

In a way she was.

Her mother-in-law looked at the car again and then

shook her head. "Well, we've planned such fun things to do, Alexandre. If your mother's made other plans, we need to tell her goodbye."

Jeanne-Marie looked at her closely. "It's not a date," she said, not wanting to hurt her mother-in-law. She did, however, have the right to see anyone she wished. And if she did start dating again, it didn't mean she'd ever forget Phillipe.

Jeanne-Marie heard a car door shut and she looked back to see Matt standing by the car. She drew in a breath. This was harder than she wanted.

"I'll pick him up tomorrow around four if that's a good time for you," she said.

"Yes. Do you want to stay for dinner tomorrow?"

"Thank you, but I'd better return to the inn. It's full and I've already taken today off." Jeanne-Marie leaned over and gave Alexandre a hug and whispered she loved him in his ear. "Be good for Grand-mère," she admonished. She'd miss this little guy. But it was important he visit often. She started back for the car.

"Bye, Mama," Alexandre called. She turned and waved.

Adrienne urged Alexandre into the house and shut the door.

Matt opened the passenger door for her. "You okay?"

"I should have thought this through. I expect she has me married off with a bunch of other children, just seeing me in the presence of another man. It was harder than I thought. I don't want her to get the wrong impression."

Once he was behind the wheel again, he looked at her. "Would that be so bad? If you married again? You're young, could marry and have more children."

"She'll have no other grandchildren but Alexandre," Jeanne-Marie said. "Though if it ever did happen, she'd still have a part in Alexandre's life. I would never take him away from them—that's one reason I'm still living here rather than back in the States. I hope she'd love any other children I had. A child can't have too many people love them."

"She probably only sees the potential of your moving away, taking her only link to her son with you."

"That's the very reason I didn't return to the States when Phillipe died. I wanted to stay where he'd lived, let Alexandre know his father's family. And mine. But mine are more likely to come to visit here than the Rousseaus are to venture to America. Anyway, I didn't mean to burden you with family situations."

"It's still early—want to stroll through the Prado Seaside Park?" he asked.

"Yes. Fresh air and no worries." It had been a long time since she had had a day solely devoted to her own pleasures and she planned to enjoy it. And her companion.

They walked along the broad pathways, dodging in-line skaters, dogs and kids running and yelling. The park felt festive with colorful awnings and canopies, all manner of items for sale at the edge, from clothes and jewelry to fresh fruit and fish. Exploring each stall didn't give time for introspection or much conversation, which suited Jeanne-Marie perfectly. By the time they were ready to find a restaurant for dinner she was feeling carefree and happy.

Waiting for a table, she glanced around. She'd never eaten in this establishment, no memories to detract from her time with Matt. Soaking up the atmosphere, she committed it all to memory—to pull out in the winter months when she might be feeling blue. She'd have this happy afternoon to remember.

The maître d' seated them at a small table to the side. Perusing the menu, Jeanne-Marie was delighted with the choices of fresh fish. She loved fish, but didn't especially like the cleaning necessary to serve it at home. She smiled when she looked at Matt.

"What's that for?" he asked, putting down his own menu.

"You've given me a wonderful day. One to remember down through the years. Thank you."

"Nothing much."

"But perfect as it was."

"Perfection is hard to reach in this day and age."

"Not always. Where will you go next on holiday?" she asked, not wanting to dwell on the future, but curious if he'd say he'd come back.

He was staying another day or two. Then he'd be returning home. Next time he took a vacation, it likely wouldn't be to a sleepy town along the Med.

"I'll go skiing this winter in Gstadd," he said. "Do you ski?"

"I used to, but haven't since Alexandre was born. I was pretty good. Skiing's popular in California."

"I enjoy it."

"No desire to climb the peaks instead of skiing down them?" she teased.

He caught her gaze and held it. "I'm not completely devoted to climbing as I think Phillipe was. I like a variety of sports. Besides, climbing in winter could be very dangerous."

"Instead of only sort of dangerous?" she asked.

"Exactly." He shrugged and leaned back slightly, his gaze firmly on her.

The waiter came to take their order. When he left, Matt asked about her own plans for the rest of the summer.

"I have full bookings through August. Once school begins, visitors taper off. Until the Christmas break."

"Will you take a holiday in the fall?" he asked.

"Maybe, but just for a weekend. Last year we went up to Paris. I wanted to show Alexandre where his mother and father met. Now I'll be one of the families limited to traveling around a child's school schedule."

"Tell me your favorite place in Paris."

She smiled and told him about the Tuileries Garden and how often she and Phillipe had gone there. How last fall she'd shown her son all their favorite spots so he'd have some knowledge of his father's life. That led to reminiscences about their respective childhoods. The meal was served. The conversation continued, with each learning more and more about the other.

When it was time to leave, Jeanne-Marie did so with reluctance. Her special day was ending. She wished she could hold back time.

The drive back to St. Bartholomeus was quickly made, with little traffic on the highway. The inn looked especially welcoming with lights spilling from the large French doors onto the veranda. Her student employee had his nose in a book, as usual, when they walked into the lobby.

Rene looked up, blinking as if not sure where he was. "Home already?" Glancing at the clock, his eyes widened slightly. Jeanne-Marie looked as well; it was almost midnight. Much later than she expected.

"I'm sorry we're so late. No problems?"

"None." He put a bookmark between the pages and stood.

After he left, Matt looked at her. "I'll be leaving early on one last climb tomorrow. Breakfast at six-thirty?"

"Yes. Thank you again for a lovely day."

"I enjoyed myself, as well," he said. Then he kissed her.

She had been half expecting it—or hoping for it? She hoped all her guests were already in and not likely to walk through the lounge as she moved closer, thrilled when his arms came around her to draw her against him. His hard body pressed against her while his mouth wreaked havoc with her senses. She encircled his neck and kissed him back, reveling in the sweet sensations that seemed to lift her from the present into a dream time. A wonderful ending to a wonderful day.

She would not think about tomorrow being his last day. She would not think about the empty days ahead. She would not think about anything but the way his kisses made her feel.

Time seemed to stand still. The lights in the lounge faded. She was floating on passion and desire, hungry for more, buoyed by the waves of ardor of his kiss and the fervor of her own.

When he pulled back a scant inch, it was to ask, "Do you have to go to bed right now?"

She looked up at him. "What do you have in mind?" Her heart pounded. What would she say if he asked her to his room? She wasn't sure she was ready for that. Yet the way she felt, she was equally uncertain whether she could refuse.

"A midnight swim?"

The cool sea might be what was needed to keep her blood from boiling. This time there would be no little boy to chaperone. She smiled dreamily. "I think that sounds very daring and unlike me. Twice in a week! Yes, I'd love to join you there."

"Meet me back here in five minutes." He gave her a quick kiss.

"Okay." Another quick kiss.

She stepped back but he wouldn't let her go until he'd given her another kiss.

"Hurry," he urged.

Jeanne-Marie didn't need any encouragement. She didn't want to miss a minute with Matt.

Wading out into the water a few moments later, she felt young and carefree. Around the curve of the beach, close to the heart of the village, other revelers were playing in the water. Their laughter and shouts could be heard in the otherwise silent night. All the establishments along the beach were brightly lit as the celebration continued far into the night.

They swam side by side until the sound of the merriment in town faded. The gentle breeze refreshed. The water was cool, but not unduly so. It felt silky against her sensitized skin. Every sense was heightened just being with Matt.

"I don't have this at home," he said when they stopped swimming, lazily moving their arms to keep upright in the buoyant sea.

"And I don't usually come out after dark. It's magical. I love looking at the lights on shore and seeing them reflected on the water."

"You make the evening magical," he said, swimming closer.

Tentatively she reached her foot down. It was too deep to stand. If she could, would he kiss her again?

"Let's head back," she suggested, hoping when they

reached standing depth he'd want to do more than return to the inn.

They swam toward the beacon of the inn. When she reached waist-high water, she stood up and began wading toward the shore, leaning to one side to wring the water from her hair.

When she straightened, Matt was there. He brushed some of the hair back from her face, then cupped it and leaned in to kiss her. His palms were warm against her cheeks and his mouth a delight against hers. Stepping closer, she pressed against him, feeling the coolness of his skin heat where hers touched until it instantly turned hot. He wrapped her in his arms and held her closely. Skin to skin, mouth to mouth, she was in heaven. She felt the gentle movement of water move to shore and retreat, but only in an abstract way—her entire being was enveloped by Matt.

Longings and desire rose. She wanted this man. She didn't question falling for someone so fast. She could easily fall totally in love with Matt and be heartbroken when he left. But she couldn't stop their kisses if she tried. She couldn't stop her heart from opening to him, and wanting him with an intensity that startled her.

His mouth trailed kisses along her jaw and she tilted back her head to give him access to her throat. Hot kisses along the pulse point at the base, then back up to her mouth again. Her tongue danced with his. The heat seemed to escalate until she vaguely wondered if the sea temperature would rise.

His chest was muscular and hard against hers. His arms held her securely, firmly, lovingly. He was no more immune to the passion rising than she.

A passing speedboat raised a wake that washed them up to their shoulders, breaking the moment as they struggled for footing against the water's surge. She stepped back, laughing and breathing hard. Trying to see him in the dim light was difficult. He was merely a silhouette. But she knew he was there. Where did they go from here?

"I should go in." She needed to get ready for the morning. But she didn't want to leave him. Yet she knew she was not ready for the next step. Not that he'd said anything to indicate he wanted a next step.

"Morning comes early, I know." He turned and started walking toward their towels.

Disappointed, Jeanne-Marie followed. She dried off, wrapped her hair in the towel and donned her cover-up.

He had toweled off as well and pulled on a T-shirt.

Taking several steps toward the inn, she realized he wasn't going with her. She turned. "Good night, Matt. Thank you again for today."

He stood near the water's edge, barely visible.

"Good night, Jeanne-Marie. It was a good day, wasn't it?"

She caught the hint of surprise in his voice. "It was." She turned and walked back to the inn and straight through to her private quarters, her heart racing. She licked her lips, tasting salt water and Matt. When she shut the door behind her, she shook her head trying to dislodge the desire that simmered. They had no business kissing like that. She knew there was no future with them.

But, oh, for a moment she could dream of them sharing kisses well into the future.

Matt watched her go with some regret. He clenched his hands into fists, wishing he knew what was going on.

Her soft body inflamed him. Her guileless gaze when she looked into his eyes caused his own common sense to flee. Her mouth was sweetness and passion.

He had enjoyed the day. That was a minor miracle in itself.

Kissing her had driven all thought from his mind. Now sanity returned.

She was nothing like Marabelle, but she was gradually pressing out his memories of his wife.

Panicked, he turned and began walking toward the cliffs, leaving the inn, the town and the partygoers behind. The faint moonlight of a waxing moon gave enough illumination. His thoughts were torn. He couldn't forget Marabelle. She'd been his life's love. And his son. The ache of their loss would never go away.

Yet as he walked, he could hear the echo of Jeanne-Marie's laughter. See the way her eyes sparkled when they dodged that one kid on the bike who'd almost ran into them. She hadn't gotten angry, but excused him for his youthful exuberance. And commented on how agile they'd been. She'd been enthusiastic about the entire day, including the meal they'd shared before returning to St. Bart.

It had been a good day. Not what he'd expected when he'd come to climb the cliffs. For two years he'd lived in a kind of limbo. Today, he'd been involved.

When he reached that section of shoreline where rocks tumbled from cliffs above him, he turned to retrace his steps. He'd take one last short climb in the morning, then head for home.

Thoughts of home, of the work awaiting, began to crowd in. The break had been welcomed, but he had the company to run. It was time to end the holiday and return to his life.

* * *

Matt entered the kitchen the next morning, his mouth watering at the aroma that filled the air. Jeanne-Marie was baking cinnamon rolls and he could almost taste them from the cinnamon scent alone.

"Good morning," she said, scarcely looking up when he walked over to the counter where she was filling another pan. "Hot chocolate will be ready in a moment," she added.

"Good morning to you. I can pour my own hot chocolate if you like," he said, watching her. He'd like to kiss her, but wasn't sure if she'd welcome the gesture in the midst of working. If they didn't stop at one kiss, breakfast could be seriously delayed.

At her nod, he reached for a mug and poured the hot beverage. Leaning against the counter he studied her as she worked. It was like poetry in motion. Her hands rolled the dough, then swiftly cut it into strips to coat with the cinnamon spread and roll into tight wheels. They would expand when baked. Her concentration was complete.

"Can I help in any way?" he asked.

"No. Sit. I'll bring you a roll as soon as the first batch comes from the oven in about three minutes." With that she darted a glance in his direction, then looked instantly back at the task at hand.

"It's supposed to rain this afternoon," she said. "I would suggest being off the cliffs when the storm comes."

Matt nodded. He knew better than she how dangerous wet rock could be. If lightning was in the mix, storms could become lethal.

Despite his best efforts, she would not be drawn into conversation, remaining firmly behind the counter preparing the rolls, then moving to another kind of bread.

At that rate she'd have enough bread to feed the entire town of St. Bart.

Feeling vaguely dissatisfied, and yet unable to pinpoint exactly why, he left once he'd finished eating. She'd prepared him another box lunch, which he stuffed into his backpack before he headed out. The dawn sky was luminescent in pale pink. He found a short route to a ledge he'd try for today, eat one last time on Les Calanques, then pack and head for home.

The appeal of climbing had waned, he admitted as he stood at the base of the faint track left from previous climbers and considered the best route up. He would rather have spent the day with Jeanne-Marie, even if they just sat on the beach and talked. Though if it were to rain later, that probably wouldn't be feasible. Sitting together in the lounge, maybe lighting a fire in the fireplace to chase away the chill, talking, learning more about her wouldn't be bad, either.

"Forget it," he muttered, reaching out for the first protrusion and raising his body up with fingertips and toeholds only.

It took less than three hours to reach the ledge. An easy climb, just as he'd wanted for this last day. He stretched out on the narrow lip and pulled out the lunch she'd made. Still early to eat, he nevertheless munched the fresh bread, cheese and grapes. Already he was changing from vacation mode to business mode as he began to itemize all the things he needed to look into upon his return to work.

He looked toward St. Bart. He couldn't see the inn from this vantage point, but could see the farther end of town as it curved into the sea. Boats sailed in the water, which was more a steely-gray today than the normal blues and aquas. He studied the overcast sky. It looked as if it would start raining earlier than predicted. Finishing rapidly, he made sure he left no trace and began to descend, trying a different route for variety.

The first raindrops hit before he was halfway down the face. Seconds later a deluge poured down on him, water running down the face of the cliff, running into his own face, blinding him as it splashed into his eyes. Dusting his hand with resin only to have it turn to paste when it got wet did not give him the secure purchase he needed on the rock face. He made an extra effort for speed while not sacrificing safety. Maybe he should have remained on the ledge until the storm had passed. Waiting would ensure water wouldn't be sheeting on the rock, making each hold more treacherous than before.

Not able to wipe the water from his face, he shook his head again and again to clear his vision. Not that he saw much—wet rock, gray skies and, if he glanced down, the waiting rocky ground.

When he was about twenty feet from the base, he lost his footing. For a moment he hung by his fingertips, searching for a toehold to keep him in place. One foot found a tiny knob. Adrenaline spiked. He took a breath, feeling his fingers slip. The knob gave way. For an instant he stared dumbfounded at the rock face, slipping past him at an astonishing rate.

A split second of pain, then blackness.

CHAPTER EIGHT

THE RAIN CAME so hard it almost obliterated the sea as Jeanne-Marie sat at the registration counter catching up on bills and receipts. Once it began, it was as if the storm settled in over St. Bart. It poured for hours, a hard driving deluge. She hoped Alexandre was enjoying his visit and wondered briefly what his grandparents would do with him in the rain. From time to time she glanced up, wondering where Matt was. He couldn't still be climbing. He was too experienced to try it in this downpour, so he was probably holed up somewhere to wait out the rain.

It was almost time for her next guests to arrive. Too bad they were coming on a day like today. The beauty of the village and sea were hidden in the rain. It looked close to twilight, though it was still midafternoon. She would be leaving to pick up Alexandre as soon as Rene arrived.

She heard a car on the gravel of the parking lot and checked things around her. Everything looked warm and welcoming with scattered lights on. She took a registration card from the stack and placed it and a pen on top of the counter.

To her surprise a police officer entered. Suddenly her heart dropped. She blinked as fear flooded. She'd been through this once before. Mesmerized by the officer's solemn look, she tried to breathe but felt her breath catch in her throat. Matt—something had happened to Matt. No, please, not that!

"Madame Rousseau," the police officer greeted her. "One of your guests is a Matthieu Sommer, *n'est ce pas?*"

"Yes. He has a room here." She couldn't say anything else as her heart raced. *Please don't let him tell me Matt died,* she prayed.

"He was in an unfortunate accident today—he fell while climbing. He's being transported to a hospital in Marseilles. He asked to have you notified."

Her worst fear—yet not quite. He had not died from the fall. She had to catch her breath.

"Ah, then he's alive."

"*Oui,* and not happy from what I heard. But he did not wish you to worry when he didn't return today."

She gave a brief prayer of thanks and tried to smile. But the fear that coursed through her had her blinking back tears instead. "Thank you for letting me know. Is he badly hurt?" she asked. How far had he fallen? What had happened?

The man checked the small notebook in hand and nodded. "Broken arm plus scrapes and bruises and a concussion. He won't be climbing again for a while."

"Thank you for letting me know," she said to the officer. Her fear diminished only slightly. A concussion wasn't good. And a broken arm would slow him down. She couldn't imagine him injured. He was in such great shape.

The officer touched the brim of his hat and turned to leave. Then he turned back. "St. Mary's Hospital. On Girard Street."

"Thank you."

The police officer was crossing the veranda when the new guests showed up. Looking surprised and curious, they entered the inn. It took only a few moments to explain his visit, register them and show them to their room. Jeanne-Marie went through the motions like a zombie. Her every thought was with Matt. She had to go see him, to verify for herself that he was alive and going to recover. She didn't question why she felt that compulsion; she just knew she had to see him.

When she came back downstairs, she yearned to pick up the phone and call the hospital. It was highly unlikely they'd tell her anything. She needed to see him for herself. But she couldn't leave before Rene arrived.

Matt's fall was her worst fear. Made more immediate with the feelings that were growing. She didn't want to care for anyone the way she had Phillipe, but Matt had become so dear to her, so important, now she knew love had slipped in unawares. She pressed against the ache in her chest. Every instinct urged her to his side. Damn the responsibilities she had to see to first. She could hardly think of what they were, so intent was her longing to get to him.

She wanted to see him, touch him, reassure herself he was alive and would be all right. Looking at the clock she seethed with impatience. Rene wasn't due for another forty-five minutes. She didn't know if she could wait that long. Her poor Matt. She hoped he wasn't in much pain. Surely they'd give him some medication for any pain. How could there not be pain, he'd fallen off a cliff!

Or could they medicate with a concussion? She didn't know—only that she had to get to him as soon as she could.

Rene arrived promptly at three.

Two minutes later she relinquished the front desk and hurried to her car. She was going to see for herself that Matt would be all right.

The drive to Marseilles seemed to take forever. Each mile mocked her with the distance between them. It was nothing to the distance once he returned home. She'd deal with that later. Right now she needed to see him.

When she reached St. Mary's, she dashed in and asked for his room.

"He's still in surgery," the receptionist said after checking. "They had to pin the arm and stitch up some cuts. He'll be in recovery soon. Are you a relative?"

"No. But a very concerned friend," she said. "I really need to see him."

The receptionist nodded. "Second floor, west. There's a surgery waiting room there and you'll be called when he's conscious again."

She was closer, but still not with Matt. Jeanne-Marie took a chair in the waiting room, staring dumbly at the television that played softly in the corner. She saw nothing but images of Matt lying at the bottom of a cliff. She wanted to see him!

Who had found him? How had they gotten him to an ambulance? How badly was he injured if he needed surgery? The minutes seemed to drag by. Questions flooded. There was so much she needed to know.

"Madame Rousseau?" A nurse stood in the doorway.

"Yes." Jeanne-Marie jumped up.

"You can see Monsieur Sommer. In fact, he's asking for you."

She followed the nurse to Matt. He was hooked up on tubes, his right arm in plaster, cuts and bruises all over his skin, with a white bandage across an area from above his ear to above his left eye. A couple of stitches on his cheek and another set on his left arm.

"What happened?" she said, going to stand right by his bed, reaching out to take his free hand, gripping it in her need to feel him, to know he was alive. "That police officer scared me to death. I thought for a second—" She wasn't going to say it. He was alive. He would be all right eventually.

"Sorry." He was slightly groggy, staring at her with eyes darkened with pain.

"I'm just glad you're going to recover. You are, right?"

"So they tell me." He frowned. "I didn't mean to fall. I didn't. Maybe I wouldn't have cared a year or so ago, but not now. I didn't mean to fall."

She squeezed his hand gently, nodding. "Of course you didn't. It's okay. You're going to be all right and back to climbing in no time." Her heart squeezed in sorrow. She knew how hard it was to go on when a loved one died. She would never ever think of Matt trying to end his life. But he might have felt that if chance had him falling, it was meant to be. She was so glad he no longer felt that way.

He closed his eyes a minute, then opened them. "My head hurts, my arm's throbbing, I ache all over. I banged up one knee."

"But you're going to be fine, give it time."

He closed his eyes again.

"I'll leave you to get some rest," she said, not wanting to go, but knowing he needed rest to heal. She could leave, having seen him. She didn't want to, but she could.

His hand gripped hers tighter. "No, don't go. It's just

I'm seeing double, so it's easier not to have my eyes open." He looked up at her. "I don't think I'll fall asleep just yet. They just woke me up from the anesthesia."

"Five more minutes, then we're taking him to his room. You can visit there," the nurse said, coming to his bed and reaching out to gently dislodge Jeanne-Marie's hand so she could take his wrist in her hand. "How do you feel?" she asked, checking his pulse.

"Like I fell off a cliff," he muttered.

Jeanne-Marie hid a smile. Grumpy she could handle. Some of her fears eased. She wanted to believe he'd be better in no time. Or as long as it took for his arm to heal. She hoped there would be nothing lasting from the fall. She couldn't bear to think of him as incapacitated in any way.

When the nurse left, Jeanne-Marie took his hand again and squeezed it gently. "Oh, Matt, you could have been far more injured or worse."

"Hey, I could have but I wasn't. The storm came in earlier than I expected. I was almost to the bottom. Short fall. I didn't mean to, truly!"

"I know."

He stared up at her for a moment. "It's important you know that."

"I do know it. Close your eyes and rest. I'll stay a bit longer."

While Matt was being moved to a private room, Jeanne-Marie went to call the Rousseaus to let them know she would pick Alexandre up later than originally planned. Then she went to find Matt's new room.

She peeped around the door and saw him lying in the hospital bed in the pristine room. The rain continued outside the window. His precious face was battered, scraped and bruised. His right wrist had a bandage around it. When he turned to see who had entered, she saw both eyes were growing black.

He smiled when he saw her and her heart flipped over. He looked as if he'd been in a fight—with the other guy winning.

"You stayed," he said.

"I said I would," she replied, coming in, pulling the visitor's chair near the bed and sitting. That put her slightly below him. She hungrily searched his face, noting the damage, thankful he was still alive. Unwilling to examine feelings that had been on a roller coaster since she received the news, she smiled and asked, "Feeling any better?" Wishing she dared reach out to touch him as she had earlier, she clenched her hands in her lap. To Matt, she was merely a friend nearby when he was injured.

"Worse than before, actually. The more the anesthesia wears off, the more I feel every inch. And all of me aches to one degree or another," he said with a wry smile. His gaze never left hers. It was as if he were drawing strength from her.

"What does the doctor say?"

"The doctor says the headache will go away and so will the double vision, but they're not sure exactly when."

"Close your eyes. You can talk with them closed."

He gave a half smile. "Guess I can," he said, closing both eyes.

"So when can you be released?" she asked.

"In a couple of days, depending on what happens with the concussion. And then only if I have a place to go where someone can watch me. Damn inconvenient, if you ask me."

"So you'll be going home?" Of course he would. Sick people liked the comfort of their own homes while recuperating.

"I don't know. It'd be a long ride. Right now I don't feel like sitting up, much less doing it for hours on end."

The silence stretched out. He was so still, she wondered if he'd fallen asleep. She didn't want him to return home. She wanted him to stay with them.

Then she said, "You could stay in Alexandre's room. He has twin beds, not the biggest in the world, but I think you could manage."

"Thanks for the thought, but I don't think I'm going to be the best patient in getting well."

She laughed. "What man is? Still, it might be better for you than going home alone. I mean, if you want to. I know Alexandre can be talkative, but I could keep him away. And you could sit on the veranda during the day and see the other guests. Read. Do whatever you want until you feel up to the long ride home."

He opened his eyes and looked into hers. "I'd be an extra burden. You said you had your life just as you liked it."

"It wouldn't be that much. I'd be happy to do it." Her heart began to race knowing just how happy she'd be to do it. She loved him. Anything to help would be a joy. And he'd stay just a little longer. She wouldn't have to say goodbye so soon.

She stared at him, her heart pounding. She loved Matthieu Sommer. Oh dear, when had that happened?

"I'd have to pay my own way."

Jeanne-Marie recognized pride when she saw it. "Fine. Maybe I'll charge in a bit extra for the waking service." She was on tenterhooks in case he realized her feelings. Had she given herself away? Only by dashing to his side when he was hurt. Please let him think of that only as a kindness.

She loved Matthieu Sommer and he had never given her any encouragement—except for those hot kisses, the joyful days at the fete and in Marseilles, and being so kind to her son.

Closing his eyes again, he nodded. "Works for me."

She considered that, knowing she'd never charge him for anything she could do for him. "What arrangements will you need?"

"I'll check with the doctor as to when he'll release me and for any special instructions. Probably say I shouldn't go climbing again for a while."

"Wise advice," she said. Why was she destined to fall in love with men who risked life and limb for a fleeting challenge of rocks and height? She looked at him and her heart melted. She caught her breath, realizing if he'd hit his head harder, if he'd fallen from a greater height, she could have lost him forever.

Not that she had him. He would be returning home as soon as he was able.

Then what was she going to do?

He opened one eye. "Thank you for coming, Jeanne-Marie."

She smiled, her heart turning over. "I wouldn't have stayed away for anything." And she hoped he never knew the full truth of that.

Just then a man knocked on the half-opened door and entered.

"Whoa, surprise, surprise. I rushed over here thinking you'd be at death's door, and here you are entertaining a pretty woman. Maybe I should fall off a cliff," he said, smiling at both Matt and Jeanne-Marie.

"Paul, what are you doing here? I thought you left for home already," Matt said.

"Couldn't resist the nightlife here, plus we only did one climb together. I called to see if you wanted to do another together before heading home and learned you were here. I couldn't head for home until I made sure you didn't need anything. I see you don't." He grinned at Jeanne-Marie.

"This is Jeanne-Marie, hostess of the inn I'm staying at. Jeanne-Marie, my climbing buddy, Paul Giardanne," Matt said.

"Explains why you didn't bother staying in Marseilles. *Enchanté, mademoiselle,*" Paul said.

"It's Madame Rousseau." Jeanne-Marie rose and nodded to Matt. "I'll call later for an update. In the meantime, rest and get better. Nice to meet you, *monsieur.*"

"Wait. Paul won't stay long." Matt glared at his friend.

"Not at all. Just wanted to make sure you were alive and kicking. Which I see you are. I'll be in town a couple more days. Do you need anything?"

"No. I'm good. Or will be once my arm heals."

"And the assorted scrapes and bruises. Man, did you slide down the face?"

"Feels like it."

Jeanne-Marie didn't know whether to stay or go. He'd asked her to stay, but if his friend visited for long, she wouldn't be needed.

"Okay, then. I'll check back tomorrow. I'll come when you don't already have company. Take care, man. *Madame.*" He bid them both goodbye.

"I could have left and let him visit with you," Jeanne-Marie said, standing by the bed.

Matt reached out to take her hand in his left one.

BARBARA MᴄMᴀʜᴏɴ   149

"I'd rather visit with you. What time are you picking up Alexandre?"

"Later. After I leave here."

"How did you fare without him around?"

"I missed him, of course. But he was only gone overnight and last night I had plenty going on." Had it only been last night they'd gone swimming in the sea, kissed in the shallows?

She sat gingerly on the edge of the bed, conscious of his hand holding hers, his thumb tracing patterns against her skin. Her heart skipped a beat. She watched him as he closed his eyes again, wishing she could soothe his headache, erase all his pain. She'd be devastated if anything happened to him. She couldn't go through something like that again.

"So tell me what exactly happened," she said.

Listening to him talk about the slippery rock and how close he had been to the bottom did nothing to alleviate her fear. When he talked about how short a time he estimated he lay at the bottom until other climbers found him, she gave up a prayer of thanks. He could have been lying in the rain for hours if they hadn't arrived.

Learning of Matt's accident had scared her to death. Maybe it was best for him to return home. At least she could always think of him alive and well and not be hurt herself when he hurt, not be worried about him if he was late coming home.

Jeanne-Marie did not tell the Rousseaus about Matt's fall and her visit to St. Mary's. They welcomed her as they always did, and Alexandre was full of talk about his playing in the room that had once been his dad's and the ice cream cone Grand-père had bought him when they went out. He could talk nonstop, she knew. But better to fill the time with that than have them question her about Matt. She would always consider them dear relatives, Alexandre's grandparents. But she also realized she was a separate person, who would have to live her life on her own terms, not those of her in-laws.

They wouldn't understand her falling in love with someone else. Not yet. Maybe never. So she kept that secret to herself.

Soon after stopping, Jeanne-Marie and her son were on their way back to the inn. It was during the car ride that she told him Matt had been injured and would be coming to stay with them a short time until he felt better.

How long did a concussion take to heal?

Alexandre was concerned about the fall and peppered her with questions. He wanted to go see him, but they were almost home by then.

"You'll see him when he comes," she ended, not able to answer more than half his questions. "He's going to share your room, so you have to be extra careful to be quiet when he's sleeping. And don't leave your toys on the floor where he can trip over them."

"I will be the bestest boy ever!" he vowed.

She laughed. "You already are."

Two days later Matt called to say he could be discharged if she was still willing to have him stay. Jeanne-Marie insisted she was. They had spoken on the phone a couple of times each day, but she had not returned to Marseilles. There was too much going on at the inn to take another day away.

She'd gone back and forth in her mind over the last two days, worried she was going to get involved more than was wise if he stayed. Yet how much more in love could she fall? She'd savor every moment together. She wanted to see him.

His room had been cleared and was now occupied by an older couple from Nantes. She already saw him in her mind every time she walked into the kitchen. Staying with them for a while—how long, days? Weeks?—would leave lasting memories of every space in the inn. Still, he'd be there a little longer. Right now, that's all that mattered.

Matt made the trip to the inn that afternoon without much discomfort. He wished he could have made it in a car, but the ambulance was comfortable and he knew the driver and paramedic would be able to convey him to the inn with minimum effort. His arm ached and his headache was relentless, pounding in time with his heart. He had trouble eating with his right arm in the cast. Closing one eye helped in the vision department, but with both closed he only felt a slight dizziness. He needed his head to heal first! This was driving him crazy.

But none of it mattered. He was going to Jeanne-Marie's until he was better. At least until the concussion healed. Which one doctor estimated might be as long as a couple of weeks. Two more weeks to hear her laugh, see her brown eyes look into his. And in the evenings after Alexandre went to bed, who knew what might happen?

The men got him out of the ambulance and into the wheelchair he'd be using until his balance stabilized. He wore a new set of clothes Paul had brought for him. A bag held his climbing gear. The gravel parking lot was bumpy, but once on the stone pathway the ride smoothed out. He wasn't complaining; at least he was away from the hospital. And almost home.

He smiled wryly. This wasn't his home. But it felt

the closest to anything home should feel like in a long time.

Entering the lobby, Matt looked around and felt a pang of disappointment. Rene was behind the desk. He looked up, startled to see the paramedics pushing the wheelchair.

"Wait there," the young man said and swiftly ran around the counter and back to the door to the Rousseaus' apartment.

In only seconds Jeanne-Marie hurried out, followed by Alexandre.

"You're here," she said, wiping her hands on the apron around her waist. "I didn't expect you this early." She smiled and went to touch his shoulder. Matt wished she'd kiss him, but with everyone standing around staring at them, she probably didn't feel it was appropriate.

He was surprised at the disappointment.

Alexandre came to his other side, looking at his chair and then at him. "You have black eyes," he said. "Do they hurt?"

"Not as much as my arm," Matt said, feeling a bit better for seeing the little boy.

Alexandre studied the cast, then smiled. "I can draw a happy face on it if you like."

Matt's arm ached and his head pounded so badly he could hardly stand it. Still, he appreciated the boy's thought. "Sure, maybe later, okay?"

The paramedics checked to make sure he had all his belongings, then left.

"Are my clothes up in my room?" He looked at Jeanne-Marie.

She shook her head. "I've already brought them down to Alexandre's room. Maybe you should rest before dinner. I can come get you when it's time to eat. Or would you rather go to bed? I bet the trip was tiring."

The spark of interest at the thought of her helping him dress for bed proved he was not as badly injured as he thought. His mind immediately envisioned the two of them alone by the bed. Only, the clothes didn't get put on, but came off.

He groaned.

"Oh, no, what hurts?" she asked, leaning close to study his face.

He opened one eye and looked at her. Could he pull her into his lap and give her a kiss?

The pain meds were messing with his mind.

"A rest would be good. I didn't realize how bumpy that highway was until I felt every jarring inch of it."

Alexandre patted his arm. "I'm sorry you got hurt," he said.

Jeanne-Marie looked him over with a critical eye. "You look exhausted behind these colorful bruises dotting your face."

"They're purple," Alexandre offered helpfully.

Matt laughed, wincing when the pain in his head upped a notch.

"Your bed's ready now. Lie down for a while. Then we'll see if you want to get up for supper or have it there. I was planning soup again."

"Sounds good to me. I don't have much of an appetite, probably due to the medication. And eating isn't the easiest thing."

"Me and Matt can sleep together in my room," the little boy said.

"I think maybe for the first couple of nights you'd better sleep in with me."

"But I want to sleep with Matt," he protested. "There're two beds. And I'll go right to sleep at bedtime. He wants me to sleep in with him, don't you, Matt?"

"Let him sleep in there, Jeanne-Marie," Matt said,

unable to resist those pleading little-boy eyes. He wondered if he objected, would Jeanne-Marie consider letting *him* sleep in with her? Sounded like a better plan all around.

"We'll see how it goes," Jeanne-Marie said.

"Did you have fun at your grandparents'?" Matt asked Alexandre. Now that the anticipation had worn off, he was tired. He was pushing things, but he wanted to be safely ensconced in bed before letting down his guard. He wasn't sure he'd be able to get up again today.

"Yes. I got to have ice cream and go for a ride with my grand-père. And swinged on the swing in the backyard. I played with my cars and we watched my dad on TV 'cause it was raining."

"Your father was on TV?"

Alexandre nodded. "It's DVDs. He smiled a lot. I like him."

"Of course you do," Matt said, wondering how it would be to have only a DVD of his dad. His father had died only a few years ago. Matt was thirty-two and he still felt he'd had his dad for too short a time. How awful would it have been to lose him before he could even remember him?

"Do you have DVDs of your dad?" Alexandre asked, leaning against his leg.

Matt nodded. "A few, with my wife and son."

"Does your arm hurt? And your face? Your eyes are dirty, they're all black."

"Everything hurts."

"Maybe Mama should kiss and make it better. She does that if I get hurt," Alexandre said very solemnly.

Matt smiled in spite of himself. He looked at her. He wouldn't mind Jeanne-Marie kissing him until he was better. It would take a lot of kisses for him to feel better.

"Let's go. We'll talk kisses later," she said, taking hold of the handles on the wheelchair.

"Deal." Matt closed his eyes as she told Rene she'd be in the back if he needed anything, and then pushed the chair.

"Do you need help getting into bed?" she asked a moment later when she stopped in the middle of the two twin beds in Alexandre's bedroom.

Matt opened one eye and surveyed the distance. Lying down would be a relief.

He made an effort and was prone on the comfortable mattress in only seconds, feeling the tension fade as fatigue won.

"I'll probably sleep through the night."

"Except when I need to waken you to make sure you're not going into a coma. I'll check back around six to see if you want to eat anything."

"Fine." With his eyes closed, he didn't see her leave, but could feel how empty the room was the next minute. Slowly he gave in to sleep.

"Wake up, Matt. I'm here to check on you," Jeanne-Marie said, coming in and dimming the light sometime later.

She touched his forehead, her hand cool and soft. Slowly she trailed it off, then pushed back his hair and reached down to press her cheek against it. "No fever that I can tell," she said. "Are you awake?"

Matt breathed in the scent of her. Too bad he was injured; he could get to enjoy attention like this. When she didn't say anything for a moment, he opened his eyes. She looked worried. He hadn't meant for that.

"I'm awake. I know who the president is," he said.

She laughed softly, brushing his hair back.

"That feels good," he said, eyes closed.

"I'm wondering if I can really let Alexandre sleep in here with you. You'd do better with complete rest."

"Let's see how things go. He'd be disappointed," Matt said. He'd give a lot to keep the boy from ever being disappointed.

"Do you want to eat something? I can bring it here."

"If it's soup, put it in a mug. I can drink it." He lifted the arm with a cast. "It's hard to eat left-handed."

Jeanne-Marie went to get his dinner, wondering if she'd lost her mind offering to let Matthieu Sommer convalesce at her home. She wanted to be more than friends. She wanted him to kiss her again. Maybe even talk about the possibility of seeing each other again. She wanted him to grow to care for her. Maybe not as much as his wife, but something more than friendship.

Was she wishing for the moon?

Alexandre was thrilled to have him stay, but she was playing with fire. Every time she saw Matt—injured as he was, the bruises on his face, the scrapes on his arms—she wanted to hold him close, share her vitality to aid in healing. She wished she could hold him, kiss him, let him know she ached with the fact he was so injured.

He ate quickly and then lay back down.

"I'll wash up and be back with Alexandre in an hour or two. Sleep if you can," she said.

Once the kitchen was clean, she quickly bathed Alexandre and then helped him into his pajamas. "Quiet when we go to your room," she said. "Matt might be asleep."

He was. She whispered to Alexandre as she tucked him in bed.

"Mama, you should kiss Matt to make him all better," Alexandre whispered back.

Jeanne-Marie tousled her son's hair. "I think time will do that," she replied.

"Please, Mama."

"Okay, now go to sleep."

She crossed over to Matt, leaning over to kiss him gently on his forehead. She wished she had the right to do that all the time.

Jeanne-Marie walked through the lounge to the veranda. Hearing the sound of the sea soothed her. She sat on one of the chairs and gazed out where the water was, hoping the peace would penetrate her jumbled thoughts. Too dark to see much, she let the soft breeze caress her as she relaxed and thought about Matt. She was falling more and more in love with him despite her best efforts to resist. She didn't have only herself to consider, but her son. Alexandre didn't miss Phillipe because he'd hardly known him. But he could get attached to Matt, and when he left, it would cause great sadness. She wanted to protect her son as much as she was able.

Yet since the accident, each time she looked at Matt, she saw possibilities. And complications. More complications than she could deal with tonight. Time for bed.

She entered Alexandre's bedroom. Both were sleeping. She went to Matt and shook him gently. "Matt?" she said softly.

He groaned and opened one eye. "What?"

"Just checking on you. Do you know what day it is?"

"The day I wanted to sleep through. I'm fine, Jeanne-Marie. Go away."

She nodded and left.

Once in the night she checked on him again, and found him just as grumpy.

The next morning Alexandre didn't come for breakfast

at his regular time. Jeanne-Marie saw to her guests, then went to his room. She could hear the two of them talking before she reached the door.

"Anyone ready for breakfast?" she asked, knocking on the door before opening it.

Matt had put a couple of pillows behind him and was halfway sitting up. His cast rested on the covers. Alexandre perched on the narrow space between Matt and the edge of the twin mattress. They both looked at her when she entered.

"I'm ready, if Matt is," Alexandre said, hopping off the bed.

"I'm more than ready," Matt said. "I could eat half a dozen eggs. The sleep really helped. And being away from the hospital."

Once breakfast was over, Jeanne-Marie suggested Matt might like to sit on the veranda. It was a pleasant day and she took a couple of moments to sit beside him. Alexandre had his cars and quickly began playing near the sand.

It was an idyllic setting, one that could lead to foolish hopes of them making a family together. Only, they were her foolish hopes. Matt hadn't even tried to kiss her since he'd returned. He'd get well and leave.

And she'd be left alone again.

CHAPTER NINE

MATT HAD MOVED to one of the lounge chairs on the veranda. Sheltered from the hot sun, he could enjoy the warmth without becoming uncomfortable. It felt good to be outside. The sea washed against the shore. Alexandre talked to himself as he played with his cars. Matt turned his head slightly to look at Jeanne-Marie, then couldn't look away. The feeling of contentment slowly faded as awareness rose. Time seemed to stand still. Despite his battered body, he wanted her. He wanted kisses and caresses and to make love all night long. Being around her made his senses soar as they never had before.

Just thinking about brushing his fingertips over her soft cheek had sent spirals of desire coursing through. He wanted to pull her into his arms and kiss her as if he'd never let her go.

Finally looking away, he tried to block the temptation with thoughts of work. He'd have to check in soon. He'd planned to be back by now. The fall had been a wake-up call. He could have died. That would have been tragic. When had he changed his mind from being willing to take his chances with fate to a strong desire to live a long life?

He still missed his wife and son, but Jeanne-Marie had brought him new reasons to embrace life.

Yet one day he would grow old and die. What would happen to Sommer's Winery then? It was a legacy to the future. The Sommer family future. He had his cousins. They would take over if he was out of the picture.

But he'd like a son of his own to pass the land to. He missed Etienne. He'd thought never to have another child, but he was young enough. If he found someone to build a life with. If he dared risk his own heart.

Very quickly a new routine was established. Jeanne-Marie prepared breakfast for her guests each morning. Then she sat with Matt and Alexandre as they ate at the table in the kitchen. After cleaning the kitchen, she'd join them on the veranda where Matt spent most of the day, resting, talking, watching the sea and laughing at the nonsense Alexandre often said.

When he wasn't resting or talking with them, however, Matt was on his phone to his office. The first day he'd been there, Jeanne-Marie had overheard him talking with an aunt, reassuring her he was going to be fine, minimizing the extent of his injuries and promising to let her know when he'd be returning home.

"I need to be able to sit long enough for the drive," he'd said.

And be able to see, Jeanne-Marie thought. But he had not told his aunt that part of his injuries.

Jeanne-Marie came to cherish those hours on the veranda. Often Matt had his eyes closed, but each day he felt stronger, the headaches began to diminish and by the end of the week the double vision was a thing of the past. They talked about everything under the sun. She learned about his cousins, friends, goals for the winery. And he questioned her about her parents, siblings, friends. When he mentioned a favorite food, she made a mental note to fix it for him. When he mentioned he liked blue, she made an effort to wear blue clothes.

Alexandre relished having so much attention. He would come and lean against Matt to discuss some important aspect of his day, or clamor to know when they'd go climbing again.

"I never fall," he told Matt.

"I rarely fall," Matt returned. "It was foolish of me to go in the rain. Remember that."

"It's not raining today. Can we go today?" Alexandre asked one afternoon.

Matt raised his cast. "I can't climb until I get this off."

"And build up your strength again," Jeanne-Marie murmured. "Alexandre, you can go climbing another time. Don't pester Matt."

"I know how," he said solemnly.

"Well, you sure have more experience than you had before. But I'm not sure you know how," his mother said.

"I do. I did good, didn't I, Matt? I didn't even fall."

"You did fine."

Jeanne-Marie did her best each day to deflect the subject of climbing, though with Matt as a constant reminder, Alexandre brought it up constantly.

By the end of the week she was getting tired of his constant pressure to go climbing. It had been a mistake to let him try. Now after one successful—easy—climb, he thought he could tag along with Matt.

"Let's go swimming," she suggested.

"Can Matt go?" he asked.

"Not while he has the cast," she said.

"Then I want to stay here," Alexandre said.

"How about I go walking along the shore, and you can splash in the water and cool off?" Matt suggested.

Twice during the week, Jeanne-Marie had to let them go off without her as she'd had guests to attend to. She'd watched them walk side by side, knowing by his position that Matt was leaning over a bit to hear Alexandre. He was so good for her son.

Despite his own loss, he seemed to enjoy being with the boy.

But it was the nights that Jeanne-Marie loved. After Alexandre was in bed and Rene had left, she and Matt would sit on the veranda and talk, kiss, be foolish together. Twice they'd walked along the shore in the moonlight. His knee was no longer giving him problems, and he'd never injured his mouth.

She felt closer than ever and so in love she could hardly see straight. He'd never said anything, but surely he had to feel something. His kisses were all a woman could want. His caresses inflamed her. His words of passion set her imagination on fire.

If he had been feeling one hundred percent, would he have pushed their involvement further? She wanted more than he gave. Yet maybe he didn't feel the same way and kisses and caresses were enough.

He never spoke of the future.

And she never stopped thinking about it.

On Wednesday Jeanne-Marie received a phone call from her in-laws asking if they could come and spend the next day with Alexandre. She was happy to invite them, but after she hung up she began to worry about what they'd think when they saw Matt. She had not told them about his injuries, or that he was convalescing here.

What would they think when they found out? Keeping

it a secret now seemed awkward. It wasn't that she didn't want them to know, precisely. Well, maybe. But only to avoid any disappointment. They loved their son. She had loved him as well. But life truly did move on. She hadn't thought she would fall in love again. Or have to keep it a secret.

Phillipe had made no secret of his love for her from the first moment they met. Matt was so different.

She didn't like complications. But she was not yet confident enough to declare her love when he had not hinted himself.

Yet, could any man kiss like he did and not feel something?

On Thursday morning Adrienne and Antoine arrived at ten.

Matt was sitting on the veranda when they arrived.

They seemed surprised to see him there, but greeted him cordially. Then turned questioning looks in Jeanne-Marie's direction.

Jeanne-Marie had told him and Alexandre at dinner last night that they would be coming. And she'd admitted they didn't know Matt was convalescing at the inn.

He knew they would be even less happy to see him if they knew the thoughts he was beginning to have about their son's widow.

"We thought we'd walk around the town for a while, then have lunch and spend the afternoon together at the beach. I know he likes to build sand castles. We'll be back before dinner," Adrienne said.

"Do stay for dinner," Jeanne-Marie said.

"Or I'd be happy to take everyone out for dinner," Matt said.

Jeanne-Marie looked at him, then nodded. "That would work, too."

The older couple looked at each other. "I suppose," Adrienne said slowly, searching Jeanne-Marie's expression as if trying to see if there was anything to learn.

Jeanne-Marie gave her son a quick hug. "Mind your grandparents," she said. She smiled at Adrienne. "I know he'll be good."

"Of course, he's Phillipe's son." With that they were off.

Jeanne-Marie sighed. "He's half mine," she said to their retreating backs.

"I think the comment was made for me," Matt said.

She shrugged. She'd tried so hard to act normal around Matt. Had Adrienne picked up on her feelings? She turned and looked at him, her heart skipping a beat. She could look at him all day. And now that he was healing, his amazing good looks were resurfacing. She no longer felt a pang of sorrow at his battered face. He was bouncing back and would be as good as new before long.

The longer Matt stayed, however, the more she dreaded his departure. Could she let him go without telling him how she felt?

And if he ever came to love her, how would she tell Adrienne and Antoine?

"Jeanne-Marie?" he said, coming to stand beside her.

She smiled at him. "We have the day to ourselves," she said. "What would you like to do?"

His expression was serious. He brushed back some of her hair from her face, letting his fingers linger. "I'm going home tomorrow. I've been away too long. I only meant to be gone a week."

Her heart dropped. Clinging to the vestige of her smile, she tried to absorb the news and not wail in denial. "Of course. You do have a vineyard to run." She turned, but he caught her arm, holding her. She kept that insipid smile on her face and looked at him.

"So what would you like to do on your last day?" she asked.

"Walk around the town, maybe have lunch on the patio at Le Chat Noir, dinner at Three Sisters? It'll take me all day to drive, so I need to start early in the morning."

"Early breakfasts are my specialty." Tomorrow morning! Less than twenty-fours hours left. She couldn't bear it.

She had to wring every memory she could from the time left. And pray she wouldn't completely fall apart when he left.

"Too bad we can't go swimming. I liked that," he said, his fingers gentle against her arm. She wanted to lean into him and hold him and never let go.

"Me, too. Let me freshen up and we can take that walk."

She went to her room, closed the door and moaned in the pain. She'd known in her head he'd be leaving. But somehow she couldn't believe it. Now it was time.

Matt stayed on the veranda, gazing out at the sea. Boats sailed across the bay. He glanced at the cliffs. Maybe he'd come again to test himself against them.

He had to return home. His fall had cemented his commitment to life. Granted, he would always miss his family. But there was more living for him to do. He'd work with his cousins and build the winery up to a world renowned producer of fine French wines. He would spend more time with his aunt and uncle. His father's brother was the only link he now had to his dad.

And he would take each day as it came, see what wonders he could wring from it like Jeanne-Marie did. He owed her so much. Her and Alexandre.

He couldn't help but smile when he thought of the little boy. He was charming without knowing it. Precocious sometimes and still just a short time away from being a baby. Matt would miss him.

And he'd miss Jeanne-Marie.

"Ready," she said behind him. She'd changed into a pretty pink top that went well with the khaki pants she wore. She'd donned dark glasses against the sun's glare. He wished he could see her pretty eyes.

"Let's walk down on the sidewalks, have lunch and then come back along the sea," he suggested.

"Fine." She fell into step with him as he headed for the small town of St. Bartholomeus. The festive air from *La Fête de la Victoire de 1945* was missing. But colorful awnings still shaded sidewalk cafés. The displays in the shops were eclectic and enticing. He wanted to visit the sporting store one more time, check out some of the climbing paraphernalia. Not that he would be doing any climbing soon.

He took her hand. She laced her fingers with his. It felt right to be seeing the town one last time with her. Would she ever consider coming to see the winery?

Did he want to continue a relationship with Jeanne-Marie once he left St. Bart? He might not return for many years. There were mountains to climb, other rock formations he wanted to try.

Yet the thought of saying goodbye bothered him.

"You're sure you're ready to drive all the way home?" she asked as they walked along.

"The headaches are completely gone. Every once in a while I feel a twinge. Good reminder to focus on what I'm doing and how worse it could have been."

"Focus?"

He looked at her. "I was distracted."

"I thought the rain made the rock slippery."

"It did. What I lost sight of was how fast the storm was moving in."

"Oh."

He could tell her he'd been thinking about her. But to what end? He found himself thinking about her most of the time lately.

They window-shopped. Entered the sporting shop and browsed the climbing gear.

"Looking for anything special?" she asked.

"No, just looking. For such a small town, this is a well-stocked store."

"Caters to the reasons a lot of people come here—the sea and the cliffs."

He'd enjoyed both.

"Ready to eat?" he asked sometime later.

"Yes."

He glanced ahead; they were near Le Chat Noir. Then he spotted Madame Rousseau sitting at a sidewalk café reading a book.

"Isn't that your mother-in-law?" he asked.

Jeanne-Marie nodded. "Where're Alexandre and Antoine?" She looked up and down the street.

"I don't see them. Maybe in one of the shops?'

When they drew opposite Adrienne, Jeanne-Marie pulled her hand free and went to the low railing separating the café from the rest of the sidewalk.

"Adrienne, where's Alexandre?" she asked as soon as she was close enough for the other woman to hear.

Adrienne looked up. "He and Antoine went off. He was telling us how he could climb and I guess he wanted to show Antoine."

"They went on a climb?"

"Hardly. I'm sure they went on a gentle ramble. But Alexandre was so delighted his grand-père was here and could see how he could climb, Antoine said he'd go with him. They'll be back soon, I'm sure. It's not like he can really climb a cliff, is it?"

"He climbed a short one."

"He's only five."

"It was very easy," Matt said. "And I understand your husband is an accomplished climber. I'm sure they'll be fine." He looked at Jeanne-Marie. "Don't worry."

"Easy for you to say. What if Antoine forgets he's so little, thinks he can do more than he's capable of?"

"Antoine's hardly dressed for serious climbing," Adrienne said. "They'll be back before long. Hungry for lunch, if I know little boys."

Jeanne-Marie looked back toward Les Calanques.

"We could walk back and meet them if you like," Matt said, picking up on her uncertainty. "I'm sure they'll be fine. His grandfather knows what little boys can do."

"Antoine's been climbing for decades and never fallen," Adrienne said, glancing at Matt's cast.

"We'll eat lunch, then if he's not back, we can walk back along the main trail to meet them."

"I think we should go now," Jeanne-Marie said.

"Antoine wasn't going to climb, just see where Alexandre had climbed and spend some time with him," Adrienne said, rising and tucking her book into her large purse. "I'll go with you. We can all eat lunch together that way."

Jeanne-Marie knew Alexandre's grandfather would never do anything to harm him, but she still wanted to make sure they were both okay.

Matt reached out and she put her hand in his. That seemed so right. She ignored Adrienne's frown when she saw they'd reached for each other. Jeanne-Marie didn't have time to worry about that right now. She wanted to make sure her baby was safe.

"I'm glad you came," she murmured as they hurried down the main street heading for the cliffs.

"He'll be all right." He squeezed her hand slightly and continued their rapid pace.

"He's all I have. I can't lose him, too."

"Don't be dramatic. He'll be fine, and probably as hungry as a bear when we find him," Matt said. He knew she was scared, but he couldn't imagine the older man putting the little boy in danger. He was probably giving Alexandre some special time together by letting him show his grandfather where he'd climbed.

Jeanne-Marie wanted to race across the distance and find Alexandre, assure herself he was fine. Once they left the town behind, the pathway became rocky and uneven, slowing them down. She would not help Alexandre if she sprained an ankle. She looked at Matt.

"Your knee holding up okay?"

"I'm fine."

She couldn't help scanning the cliffs as they approached. Adrienne kept harping that Antoine wouldn't have climbed today, but Jeanne-Marie couldn't help but be fearful she'd see her son halfway up some sheer cliff, already envisioning him falling to his death as his father had. Matt was an accomplished climber and he'd fallen. How easy it would be for Alexandre to fall. *Please, God,* she prayed, *keep my child safe.*

"Where are they?" she asked. The minutes ticked by. They scoured the pathway, looking to the left and right in case Alexandre and his grandfather were off to the side. From time to time they had to scramble over rocks. Where were they? They were quite a distance now from St. Bart.

They passed others hiking back toward St. Bart and asked them if they'd seen the older man and young boy. They had not. Jeanne-Marie was sick with fear.

"Stop." Matt pulled her to a halt and waited for Adrienne to catch up. The older woman was breathing hard and now looking worried.

"I can't believe they would have come this far. We must have missed them," she said.

"We need to think this through and not rush off with no plan," Matt said. "I'd thought we'd run into them by now, but it appears they went farther than I would have."

"Or returned by the sea and we missed them," the older woman insisted, looking behind them as if expecting her husband and grandson to appear.

"Are we at the spot we climbed?" Jeanne-Marie asked. "It all looks the same to me."

"Not quite. It's just ahead."

"Then I say we go on to see if they're there."

"If the hikers didn't see them, either they left the path or they returned home before we left and we've missed them. They could have gone along the sea as Madame Rousseau said and be back at the inn wondering where we are."

"They would've gone back to Adrienne," Jeanne-Marie said. "Antoine would have taken them all to lunch."

Adrienne nodded. "I agree they'd have come for me before lunch."

"I suggest we begin looking off the main path, where there are side paths that have gentle scrambles. We have a man in his fifties and a five-year-old child. He would not take the child up the face, so they have to be somewhere on the flat, but maybe off this path," Matt said reasonably.

Five minutes later Jeanne-Marie recognized the gentle slope they'd climbed a couple of weeks ago. No sign of Alexandre. Where was he?

Then Matt stopped abruptly. "Wait, listen!"

The faint cry seemed to float in the air, directionless. He tilted his head to hear better. Jeanne-Marie almost held her breath. It was Alexandre.

Matt looked up and scanned the cliff.

"*Mon Dieu,* he's there." He indicated a point about thirty feet up the cliff a few yards beyond where they stood. Alexandre peered over a ledge. There was no sign of Antoine Rousseau.

"He climbed it again," Matt said. "I wouldn't have believed it."

"Where's Antoine?" Adrienne sounded frantic as she came up and clutched his arm. She scanned the cliff in all directions. "I don't see him."

"Alexandre, we see you. Wait there, do not move," Matt yelled up. "Wave if you hear me, but do not move from where you're sitting."

The little boy waved his hand. "I can't get down. I don't know where to put my feet. Matt, can you tell me? Grand-père is sleeping."

A small blue object flew from the ledge, bounced against some outcropping and landed at the base.

"My car!" Alexandre leaned over watching the toy bounce down the cliff.

Jeanne-Marie stared in fear. She could scarcely breathe. She wanted to fly to her child, yet her feet couldn't move. "Get back!" she screamed. She looked at Matt. "How did he get up there? How could he? The other day you had to show him every handhold."

"Apparently so did Antoine. It really is an easy climb, Jeanne-Marie. Now I'll talk you up. You've done it before. It's the same place."

"But you were with us. I can't climb this cliff." Her eyes returned to Alexandre. He seemed so little against the immense cliff. She wanted to cry. Instead Matt pulled her along to the area directly beneath the ledge. He was scanning the face, studying the rocks and crevices.

Jeanne-Marie yelled up to Alexandre, "Stay back from the edge, sweetie. We'll come get you, but move back."

"I lost one of my cars," he wailed.

"We'll find it once you get down. Get back!"

Matt needed only a second to plan what to do. "I don't see his grandfather, but something's wrong. He wouldn't take a nap. *Madame,* you must go back to the village to get help."

"No, I need to know if Antoine's all right," Adrienne said. "Alexandre, where is Grand-père?"

"He's sleeping. He won't wake up." The little boy peered over the edge.

"Get back against the cliff," Jeanne-Marie yelled. Her heart pounded with fear, her eyes unable to leave the sight of her precious little boy high above her on a rocky ledge.

"You have to go for help, *madame.* Find the constable

and tell him there's been a climbing accident. He'll bring rescue workers. Go, speed is of the essence," Matt instructed Adrienne. "Be sure to tell them we need a medic. And be careful; we can't afford to have you slowed down by being injured. I think maybe your husband had a heart attack."

"Oh, no, Antoine!"

Matt looked up again, studying the cliff face. "The sooner you bring help, the sooner we can get to him," Matt said with what patience he could muster. It was an easy climb, but still a challenge for a child. Had he been in perfect condition, he could scramble up in five minutes and bring Alexandre right back to his mother.

"I can't climb," he said aloud. "My arm will not hold my weight. You'll have to do it, Jeanne-Marie."

She turned to look at him in astonishment, tears glistening on her cheeks. "I can't climb, I'm too afraid. You have to go. He's so little. Please, Matt. I need you to rescue my son."

CHAPTER TEN

"I WOULD GIVE my fortune to be able to do that, but I can't. Not won't, but physically cannot. It's an easy climb…you've done it already. You can do it again. But it still needs both hands and feet, and my arm prevents me from going. You'll have to climb up, stay with Alexandre and wait until rescue comes. The men who come will be able to get you down with no trouble."

"I can't." She turned and looked at the cliff with horror on her face. Fear pounded through her. All she could think of was how Matt had guided her up and back the last time. She couldn't do it on her own.

He caught her chin and brought her face around to his. "Yes, you can. This is an easy climb—a five-year-old did it. You've done it. I'll guide you every inch from the ground. We'll take it slow and you'll be up with him in no time. You need to check on Antoine, too. When the rescue workers arrive, you two will be the first down. You can do this. Trust me, I would never put you in harm's way."

"If I fall, Alexandre will have lost two parents."

"Look at me. You will not fall. I can see a clear way up from here. I'll tell you every move to make."

"You know what you're doing and you fell. I have

climbed only a few times, never on my own. I could fall and get killed."

"Or you can climb up the way I tell you and be with your little boy."

She stared into his eyes, clinging with hers, as if hoping to draw confidence from his gaze. Tears stopped and a certain resolve took their place.

"I'm scared out of my mind," she said in a wobbly voice.

"I know. But you can do this. Think of Alexandre. He needs you. Trust me, Jeanne-Marie, I would never let anything bad happen to you."

"Mama, come get me," her son called.

Jeanne-Marie and Matt both looked up—Alexandre was leaning over the edge again.

"Get back, I'm coming," she yelled. Taking a deep breath, she looked back at Matt. Recklessly she pulled his head down and kissed him. "For luck," she said when she stepped back. Turning before she could change her mind, she walked to the base of the cliff. Looking up, it seemed endless. She tried to breathe, but fear clogged her throat.

"Move to your right about four feet. See the rocks jutting out from the base?" Matt asked, coming beside her and pointing to the protrusions.

"Yes," she said.

"Look here." He pointed to some others higher up. "Step up there, reach up for this one and hold on with your hand. Okay, good. Now lift your left foot and reach for the rock about ten inches up. Good. Now move your right hand up to grasp that rock a bit to your right."

Step by step he directed her through the climb. It was an easy trail, and as she climbed, she concentrated on the calm instructions Matt called. She'd done this before. She didn't find it fun, but it was not impossible. Slowly but steadily she moved up the slope.

Matt watched carefully, scouring the cliff, looking for the easiest way for her to get to Alexandre. Once her foot slipped and Matt caught his breath. She could not fall. Please God, do not let her fall. She quickly put her foot on the outcrop of rock and found a new handhold. In less than five minutes, she reached the ledge, pulled herself on it and swept Alexandre up in a fierce hug, drawing him back against the cliff that rose so high behind them, away from the edge, out of his view.

Matt turned and leaned against the wall. His heart pounded. He'd never felt such fear when he was climbing, but he worried every second that she would fall and be injured or worse. He felt he'd aged five years in five minutes. Yet she'd done it. He'd known she could.

Pushing away, he walked out several yards to look up. He couldn't see anyone, but could hear her soft voice murmuring to Alexandre.

"Is Antoine there? You two okay?" he called up.

"Yes, but he's unconscious and his color's not good. He's breathing, but his lips look blue—can't be from cold, he's in the sunshine."

Coming down would be harder than going up—especially for Alexandre. On their climb he'd been right beside the boy, ready to catch him in an instant if he missed a step. He wouldn't risk the child or the mother on their climbing down on their own. He had to bide his time until the rescue people arrived to see her safely down. God, it was terrifying when you saw someone you loved in danger.

Loved? He closed his eyes tightly. Loved. He loved Jeanne-Marie. The fear he'd felt for her safety made it all come clear. He'd been reluctant to leave; only pressing business matters had finally decided on his departure in the morning.

Now he didn't want to leave at all. Duty called. His heart had been captured again. He hadn't expected to ever fall in love again. He couldn't realize his love for her only to have her fall from a cliff. The ironic turn almost made him sick.

Her voice came down. "I've loosened his collar, but he doesn't respond when I shake him. It must be a heart attack."

"Yes. He's not in danger of falling over the edge, is he?"

He heard some scraping, then Jeanne-Marie's head peered over the edge. "I moved him back, but I don't think he's going anywhere. You remember how wide the ledge is and it has what looks almost like a shallow cave at the back. I'll try to get him out of the sun, but he's heavy, and I don't know if I'm doing any damage moving him."

"No visible injuries?"

"No. Alexandre said they just climbed up, and Grand-père was breathing hard and then lay down." She looked out across the sea. "I see the same view from my house. There's nothing special about this. I still don't see why people risk their lives."

"We can talk about that when you get down. You did a good job and I know Alexandre will forever remember his mother came to his rescue."

"Thanks to you. I'm still scared out of my mind. They'd better have ropes to get me down so I can keep my eyes closed the entire way."

He laughed, wishing he could have spared her. Wishing he could have been the one to rescue her son. As climbs went, this one was very easy.

Trying to gauge when Madame Rousseau would return with help, Matt sat on a boulder and watched the edge of the ledge wishing with all he had he could be there with them. Jeanne-Marie and Alexandre weren't to be seen, but he heard the murmur of their voices. How long would it take the older woman to convince the local Search and Rescue group to mobilize? He hoped not long.

The afternoon continued. The sun was hot. The breeze from the sea sporadic. His head began to throb again. He was not fully recovered from his own fall. What would he have done if Jeanne-Marie had fallen? He didn't want to think about that.

He wished they'd brought water. Probably Alexandre wished for food. He looked back down the path, but no sign of anyone.

Then he heard the sound of a powerful boat rounding the spit of land separating them from St. Bart's bay. In only a moment he saw several men standing on the large boat. The driver brought the boat close to shore and three men jumped out, coils of rope over their shoulders. A young policeman led the way.

With a few succinct words, Matt outlined the situation and urged them to get the woman and child down first.

Jeanne-Marie peered over the edge.

"You'll be down in no time," Matt called up.

The men were efficient, scrambling up the rock as if it were a walk in the park. And true to his word, in no time Jeanne-Marie and Alexandre were on the ground.

Matt helped them untangle themselves from the ropes that had belayed them down, then swept Jeanne-Marie into a tight hug. His chin rested on her head, his eyes on Alexandre. "You two doing all right?"

"I lost my car," Alexandre said, looking around.

"How's Antoine?" Matt asked, unable to let her go.

"The men were strapping him on the stretcher, then they'll let him down," she said, clinging as tightly as he was holding her.

They watched as the Search and Rescue men began to lower the stretcher on its journey down. Two men held the ropes at the top, one accompanied the stretcher lest it get caught on some rocky protrusion. In no time Antoine was on the ground. Jeanne-Marie and Matt went to stay with him while the other men made short work of descending.

"The boat'll be faster and easier on him," Matt said, watching as they carried the stretcher to the waiting boat.

Once aboard, the SAR men verified the three of them could make it back to St. Bart on their own, the boat pulled back and swiftly headed for St. Bart.

"Thank you," Jeanne-Marie called. "Tell his wife we'll be along as soon as we can."

"I see my car!" Alexandre exclaimed, running a short distance to pick up a blue object. Sadly he studied it and then came back. "It's broken."

"Thank God it's only the car that was broken," she said, hugging him quickly.

"I didn't fall like my dad or Matt," he said, looking up the face of the cliff. "But it was really scary, Mama, to be alone when Grand-père went to sleep. I wanted Matt with me. He's the best."

"He is, but unless he's there, you had better never climb a rock again!"

Matt took her chin in his hand and kissed her. "I was scared to death for you," he said.

"Are you kissing Mama?" Alexandre asked, coming to stand beside them both.

"I am." Matt stooped and hugged Alexandre and kissed the top of his head. "And I'm kissing you because you're safe."

"Oh." He smiled at Matt. "Are you proud of me? I showed my grand-père how I could climb. He said he was proud of me. Only then I couldn't go down."

"Going down is the hard part, remember. You were smart to stay there until a grown-up came."

"Yes, my mama!"

Alexandre reached out for her hand, Matt took the other. For a moment Jeanne-Marie was as happy as she'd ever been.

When they reached the beach, they veered off the path and walked on the damp sand. Alexandre raced ahead.

"No lasting harm, I think," Matt said, watching him.

"Kids are resilient. I may never recover, however," she said.

"Me, either," he said.

She looked at him. "Why's that? As you said, it wasn't that big a challenge. If your arm was healed, you'd probably scramble up it in a heartbeat."

"I have an entirely new perspective on things."

"What do you mean?"

"I'll tell you later." He glanced down at her and squeezed her hand slightly.

"I'm so glad you were here. You knew exactly what to do."

"I'm glad I was here as well."

The inn came into sight. Alexandre was already running up to the veranda, none the worse for his afternoon on the ledge.

"I'll need to call the clinic to see how Antoine's doing. And if he's conscious, find out what in the world he was thinking letting Alexandre climb."

"My guess, he knew the child had done it before, and he was there to supervise. If he hadn't had a heart attack, they'd have been back for lunch with Alexandre thrilled to have climbed with his grandfather. Antoine probably wanted to recapture what is now lost with the death of his son."

Jeanne-Marie called the clinic as soon as she reached the inn and learned Antoine had been stabilized and then airlifted to a hospital in Marseilles. The diagnosis was a heart attack, but he'd been awake and lucid before leaving the clinic. The hope was he'd recover fully.

Putting down the phone, she smiled tentatively at Matt, who hovered nearby.

"He's going to recover?" he asked.

"They think so. This sure isn't the vacation you envisioned, I bet."

"Hey, glad I was here. I would hate to think of you going through something like this on your own."

"I never want to think of going through another day like today."

"I'll take you and Alexandre out tonight. Le Chat Noir's your favorite, I have it on good authority."

"Then a walk back along the beach?"

"Yes." Between now and then he had some serious thinking to do.

Jeanne-Marie bathed Alexandre, then put him down for a nap, citing his busy day and the dinner in the offing that night. He was asleep in less than five minutes. She then went to take a long shower, washing away the grit and dirt, trying to wash away the memories of that horrible few minutes when she saw her son on the ledge with no apparent way to get down. She didn't want to relive the climb. Matt had seen every handhold and toehold and he'd been right; it was easy enough for a five-year-old. Still, it would never rank as a favorite hobby with her.

Matt—he'd been what she'd clung to during the climb. His voice, calm and assured. His vow he would let no harm come to her, his confidence in her ability to reach her son. He'd been there for her at the most crucial time.

She thought about him as she donned a pretty sundress. She owed him more than she could ever repay. And he deserved her best at dinner. She almost wished Alexandre could go and visit Michelle or another of her friends with children for the evening. Then she chided herself for the thought. Her precious son was safe and it would be a long while before she'd feel comfortable with him away from her.

Thoughts spiraled back to Matt. Did he mind that Alexandre would be going with them? He seemed to like him. He was always kind, always had time for him. Not many men would want to spend their vacation with a five-year-old.

There was no question Alexandre adored Matt—especially after their climb together. That had been all he'd talked about ever since that day.

Ready at last, she went out to the lounge area, disappointed not to see Matt there. She walked to the French doors and there he was, sitting on a chair near the far edge of the veranda.

"You look lovely," he said, rising.

"Thank you. I can get us some sandwiches and lemonade for lunch, if you like. To tide us over until dinner."

"Just a snack'll do. I'll come with you but let's eat out here."

They made the sandwiches together, bumping into each other, laughing, working in harmony.

Eating alfresco was a favorite part of living by the beach for Jeanne-Marie. She did it often and was pleased Matt seemed to like it as well.

Finished, replete, the heat of the afternoon making her a bit sleepy, she leaned back in her chair, content with the day and the way things had turned out. Now if she'd only hear her father-in-law was going to recover fully, everything would be perfect. Or almost perfect. Matt was leaving in the morning.

"Jeanne-Marie?"

Slowly she looked at him.

"I was going to wait."

"For what?"

"To ask you to marry me."

"What?" She sat up at that, totally shocked.

Matt rose and came to kneel by her chair. "I was going to wait until tonight when Alexandre was asleep and Rene had gone home. When it was just you and me. I love you, Jeanne-Marie. That became abundantly clear today when I couldn't scale the hill with you but felt your fear and uncertainty. The awful thought came— what if you fell? I couldn't imagine living through a loss like that again. I knew then the feelings I've felt over the last weeks were more than those for a friend. You have captured my heart. I never thought I'd love again. I never wanted to live in fear of something happening to someone else I love. But today proved I don't always get what I want."

"You never said you were starting to care for me. We haven't even dated. Are you trying to protect us or something? Did today make you think I can't cope on my own and need a keeper?"

He laughed. "No, you're the last person who needs a keeper. Today made me vividly aware that I couldn't imagine my life without you in it. I want you for my wife. I don't want to leave tomorrow without knowing you'll be part of my life. I know this is fast. We haven't known each other long. But sometimes it doesn't take long—to find the perfect life partner. I've found her and want to spend all my time with her—you."

She caught her bottom lip between her teeth, trying to assimilate all he was saying. Her heart blossomed. He loved her? She loved him. It was fast. It also felt right.

"I want to see you every day, eat your amazing breakfasts, hear your laughter, see your smile, touch your silky skin. I want you to be part of my life," he said, his eyes holding her gaze, the sincerity shining through. How could she have thought him stern? He was so wonderful she couldn't believe it.

She reached out and touched his cheek, her eyes growing moist.

"Today when you went up that cliff, all I could think of was what if you fell? What if you were hurt worse than I was? What if something happened and you died? I knew at that moment that I couldn't go on if that happened." He took her hand in his and kissed the center of her palm, wrapping his fingers around, relishing the touch of her skin, wanting more than anything to draw her into his embrace. But he wanted her answer first!

"I have a son—"

"Whom I already love. He's a precious child and I would be honored to have a hand in raising him. In the Loire Valley, here, wherever we live. Come, my love, make a family with me, grow old with me. Let me love you until the end of time."

Before she could open her mouth to give him an answer, he pulled her into his embrace and kissed her as they both tumbled to the veranda.

Jeanne-Marie felt like she was floating. She moved closer into his embrace, letting the love she'd kept hidden blossom and shine. She loved this man and he said he loved her.

"Mama, Mama, why are you on the floor kissing Matt?" Alexandre asked, running out from the lounge.

They pulled apart, sat up and looked at the little boy.

"I've asked your mother to marry me and come live with me in my castle. Would you like that?" Matt asked, opening his arm for the child to join them.

"Can I come, too?"

"Of course, I wouldn't take her without you." Matt scooped him up with his good arm and faced Jeanne-Marie. "I'm waiting to hear her answer," he told Alexandre. Both of them looked at her.

She laughed and reached out to touch Matt's face again, free to do so, knowing she could touch him whenever she wanted—forever. "I love you. I would be honored to marry you and come and live in your castle. As long as we can vacation here by the sea. And how many children do you want?"

"A houseful. No onlys for us."

"I think that can be arranged." She looked beyond him at Les Calanques and grew pensive. "I never thought I'd fall in love again." Looking at him, she smiled brightly. "But look what they brought me. How lucky can one person be?"

"Ah, *ma chère,* I'm the lucky one. I lost my family and now found a new one. One I'll love and cherish forever. You'll be the happiest woman on the earth if I can help it."

"I already am! I love you, Matthieu Sommer, and always will."

"Me, too," Alexandre said, smiling happily. "Now can you take me climbing again?"

SEPTEMBER 2011 HARDBACK TITLES

ROMANCE

The Kanellis Scandal	Michelle Reid
Monarch of the Sands	Sharon Kendrick
One Night in the Orient	Robyn Donald
His Poor Little Rich Girl	Melanie Milburne
The Sultan's Choice	Abby Green
The Return of the Stranger	Kate Walker
Girl in the Bedouin Tent	Annie West
Once Touched, Never Forgotten	Natasha Tate
Nice Girls Finish Last	Natalie Anderson
The Italian Next Door...	Anna Cleary
From Daredevil to Devoted Daddy	Barbara McMahon
Little Cowgirl Needs a Mum	Patricia Thayer
To Wed a Rancher	Myrna Mackenzie
Once Upon a Time in Tarrula	Jennie Adams
The Secret Princess	Jessica Hart
Blind Date Rivals	Nina Harrington
Cort Mason – Dr Delectable	Carol Marinelli
Survival Guide to Dating Your Boss	Fiona McArthur

HISTORICAL

The Lady Gambles	Carole Mortimer
Lady Rosabella's Ruse	Ann Lethbridge
The Viscount's Scandalous Return	Anne Ashley
The Viking's Touch	Joanna Fulford

MEDICAL ROMANCE™

Return of the Maverick	Sue MacKay
It Started with a Pregnancy	Scarlet Wilson
Italian Doctor, No Strings Attached	Kate Hardy
Miracle Times Two	Josie Metcalfe

SEPTEMBER 2011
LARGE PRINT TITLES

ROMANCE

Too Proud to be Bought	Sharon Kendrick
A Dark Sicilian Secret	Jane Porter
Prince of Scandal	Annie West
The Beautiful Widow	Helen Brooks
Rancher's Twins: Mum Needed	Barbara Hannay
The Baby Project	Susan Meier
Second Chance Baby	Susan Meier
Her Moment in the Spotlight	Nina Harrington

HISTORICAL

More Than a Mistress	Ann Lethbridge
The Return of Lord Conistone	Lucy Ashford
Sir Ashley's Mettlesome Match	Mary Nichols
The Conqueror's Lady	Terri Brisbin

MEDICAL ROMANCE™

Summer Seaside Wedding	Abigail Gordon
Reunited: A Miracle Marriage	Judy Campbell
The Man with the Locked Away Heart	Melanie Milburne
Socialite...or Nurse in a Million?	Molly Evans
St Piran's: The Brooding Heart Surgeon	Alison Roberts
Playboy Doctor to Doting Dad	Sue MacKay

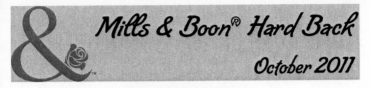

Mills & Boon® Hard Back

October 2011

ROMANCE

The Most Coveted Prize	Penny Jordan
The Costarella Conquest	Emma Darcy
The Night that Changed Everything	Anne McAllister
Craving the Forbidden	India Grey
The Lost Wife	Maggie Cox
Heiress Behind the Headlines	Caitlin Crews
Weight of the Crown	Christina Hollis
Innocent in the Ivory Tower	Lucy Ellis
Flirting With Intent	Kelly Hunter
A Moment on the Lips	Kate Hardy
Her Italian Soldier	Rebecca Winters
The Lonesome Rancher	Patricia Thayer
Nikki and the Lone Wolf	Marion Lennox
Mardie and the City Surgeon	Marion Lennox
Bridesmaid Says, 'I Do!'	Barbara Hannay
The Princess Test	Shirley Jump
Breaking Her No-Dates Rule	Emily Forbes
Waking Up With Dr Off-Limits	Amy Andrews

HISTORICAL

The Lady Forfeits	Carole Mortimer
Valiant Soldier, Beautiful Enemy	Diane Gaston
Winning the War Hero's Heart	Mary Nichols
Hostage Bride	Anne Herries

MEDICAL ROMANCE™

Tempted by Dr Daisy	Caroline Anderson
The Fiancée He Can't Forget	Caroline Anderson
A Cotswold Christmas Bride	Joanna Neil
All She Wants For Christmas	Annie Claydon

Mills & Boon® Large Print

October 2011

ROMANCE

Passion and the Prince	Penny Jordan
For Duty's Sake	Lucy Monroe
Alessandro's Prize	Helen Bianchin
Mr and Mischief	Kate Hewitt
Her Desert Prince	Rebecca Winters
The Boss's Surprise Son	Teresa Carpenter
Ordinary Girl in a Tiara	Jessica Hart
Tempted by Trouble	Liz Fielding

HISTORICAL

Secret Life of a Scandalous Debutante	Bronwyn Scott
One Illicit Night	Sophia James
The Governess and the Sheikh	Marguerite Kaye
Pirate's Daughter, Rebel Wife	June Francis

MEDICAL ROMANCE™

Taming Dr Tempest	Meredith Webber
The Doctor and the Debutante	Anne Fraser
The Honourable Maverick	Alison Roberts
The Unsung Hero	Alison Roberts
St Piran's: The Fireman and Nurse Loveday	Kate Hardy
From Brooding Boss to Adoring Dad	Dianne Drake